Andreas vented incredulity.

"Why would I lower myself to that level? Had you been my wife, I would have confronted him. I would have torn him apart for daring to lay a single finger on you!" he proclaimed. "But you're *not* my wife, you're my mistress, and as such expendable with the minimum of fuss."

Ashen-pale beneath the lash of his naked contempt, Hope looked back at him, distraught turquoise eyes sparkling with sudden angry denial. "I am not, and have never been, your mistress."

"Then what are you?" Andreas purred, like a panther ready to flex his claws and draw blood.

Harlequin Presents®

GREEK TYCOONS

They're the men who have everything— except brides...

Wealth, power, charm—
what else could a handsome tycoon need?
In the GREEK TYCOONS miniseries
you have already met some gorgeous Greek
multimillionaires who are in need of wives.

Now meet handsome, passionate and aloof
Andreas Nicolaidis in Lynne Graham's
The Greek Tycoon's Convenient Mistress

This tycoon thought he could keep
his heart protected, only to discover
that love has other plans.

Coming next month:
The Greek's Seven-Day Seduction
by
Susan Stephens
#2455

Lynne Graham

THE GREEK TYCOON'S CONVENIENT MISTRESS

GREEK
TYCOONS

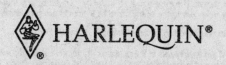

HARLEQUIN®

TORONTO • NEW YORK • LONDON
AMSTERDAM • PARIS • SYDNEY • HAMBURG
STOCKHOLM • ATHENS • TOKYO • MILAN • MADRID
PRAGUE • WARSAW • BUDAPEST • AUCKLAND

ISBN 0-373-12445-7

THE GREEK TYCOON'S CONVENIENT MISTRESS

First North American Publication 2005.

Copyright © 2004 by Lynne Graham.

Printed in U.S.A.

PROLOGUE

ANDREAS NICOLAIDIS kept a powerful grip on the steering wheel as his Ferrari Maranello threatened to skid on the icy, slippery surface of the country lane.

The rural landscape of fields and trees was swathed in a heavy mantle of unblemished white snow. There was no other traffic. On a day when the police were advising people to stay at home and avoid the hazardous conditions, Andreas was relishing the challenge to his driving skills. Although he owned a legendary collection of luxury cars he rarely got the chance to drive himself anywhere. In addition, he might have no idea where he was but he was wholly unconcerned by that reality. He remained confident that he would at any moment strike a route that would intersect with the motorway, which would enable his swift return to London and what he saw as civilisation.

But then, Andreas had always cherished exceptionally high expectations of life. He led an exceedingly smooth and well-organised existence. To date every annoyance and discomfort that had afflicted him had been easily dispelled by a large injection of cash. And money was anything but a problem.

It was true that the Nicolaidis family fortunes, originally founded in shipping, had been suffering from falling profits by the time Andreas had become a teenager. Even so, his conservative relatives had been aghast when he'd refused to follow in his father's and his grandfather's footsteps and had chosen instead to become a financier. In the years that had followed, however, their murmurs of disquiet had swelled to an awed chorus of appreciation as Andreas had soared to meteoric heights of success. Now often asked to advise governments on investment, Andreas was, at the age of thirty-four, not only worshipped like a golden idol by his family, but also staggeringly wealthy and a committed workaholic.

On a more personal front, no woman had held his interest longer than three months and many struggled to reach even that milestone. His powerful libido and emotions were safely in the control of his lethally cold and clever intellect. His father, however, had been on the brink of marrying his fourth wife. His parent's unhappy habit of falling in love with ever more unsuitable women had exasperated Andreas. He did not suffer from the same propensity. Indeed the media had on more than one occasion called Andreas heartless for his brutally cool dealings with the opposite sex. Proud of his rational and self-disciplined mind, Andreas had once made a shortlist of the ten essential qualifications that would have to be met before he would even consider a woman as a potential life partner. No woman had ever met his criteria...no woman had even come close.

Hope curled her frozen hands into the sleeves of her grey raincoat and stamped feet that were already numb.

She was hopelessly lost and there was nobody to ask for the directions that she needed to find the nearest main road. Pessimism was, however, foreign to Hope's nature. Long years of leading a very restricted life had taught her that a negative outlook lowered her spirits and brought no benefits. She was a great believer in looking on the bright side. So, although she was lost, Hope was convinced that a car containing a charitable driver would soon appear and help her to rediscover her bearings. It didn't matter that the day she had already endured would have reduced a less tolerant personality to screaming frustration and despondency. She knew that nothing could be gained from tearing herself up over things that she could not change. Yet it was hard even for her to forget the high hopes with which she had left home earlier that morning to travel to the interview she had been asked to attend.

Now, she felt very naive for having pinned so much importance to that one interview. Hadn't she been looking for a job for months? Wasn't she well aware of just how difficult it was to find employment of any duration or stability? Unfortunately she scored low when it came to the primary attributes demanded by employers. She had no qualifications in a world that seemed obsessed with the importance of exam results. Furthermore, hampered as she was by her lack of working experience, it was a challenge for her to provide even basic references.

Hope was twenty-eight years old and for more than a decade she had been a full-time carer. As far back as she could remember, her mother Susan had been a sick woman. Eventually her parents' marriage had broken down beneath the strain and her father had moved out. After a year or so, all contact had ceased. Her brother, Jonathan, who was ten years older, was an engineer. Having pursued his career abroad, he had only ever managed to make occasional visits home.

Now married and settled in New Zealand, the Jonathan who had flown in to sort out their late mother's estate a few months earlier had seemed almost like a stranger to his younger sister. But when her brother had learned that he was the sole beneficiary in the will, he had been so pleased that he had spoken frankly about his financial problems. In fact he had told Hope that the proceeds from the sale of his mother's small bungalow would be the equivalent of a lifebelt thrown to a drowning man. Conscious that her sibling had three young children to provide for, she had been relieved that their late mother's legacy would be put to such good use. Back then, she had been too ignorant of her own employment prospects to appreciate that it might be very hard for her to find either a job or alternative accommodation without a decent amount of cash in hand.

The silence of a landscape enclosed in snow was infiltrated by the distant throb of a car engine. Fearful that the vehicle might be travelling on some other road, Hope tensed and then brightened as the sound grew into a reassuring throaty roar and the car got audibly closer. Her generous pink mouth curved into a smile. Eyes blue as winter pansies sparkling, she moved away from the sparse shelter of the hedge to attract the driver's attention.

Andreas did not see the woman in the road until he rounded the corner and then there was no time to do anything but take instant avoiding action. The powerful sports model slewed across the road in a wild skid, spun round and ploughed back across the snowy verge to crash with a thunderous jolt into a tree. Ears reverberating from the horrible crunching complaint of ripping metal, Hope remained frozen to the same spot several feet away. Pale with disbelief and open-mouthed, she watched as the driver's door fell open and a tall black-haired male lurched out at speed. He moved as fast as his car, was her first embryonic thought.

'Move!' He launched at her, for the pungent smell of leaking fuel had alerted him to the danger. 'Get out of the way!'

As his fierce warning sliced through the layers of shock cocooning Hope, the car burst into flames and she began to stir, but not speedily enough to satisfy him. He grabbed her arm and dragged her down the road with him. Behind them the petrol tank ignited in a deafening explosion and the force of the blast flung her off her feet. A strong arm banded round her in an attempt to break her fall and as she went down he pinned her beneath him.

Winded, she just lay there, lungs squashed flat by his weight and struggling to breathe again while she reflected on the impressive fact that he had in all probability saved her life. She looked up into bronzed features and clashed with eyes the exotic flecked golden brown of polished tortoiseshell.

At some level she was conscious that her clothes had got very wet when she'd fallen, but the damage was done and it seemed much more important to recognise why those stunning eyes of his struck such a chord of familiarity with her. As a child she had visited a zoo where a splendid lion had been penned up behind bars, which he had fiercely hated and resented. Tawny eyes ablaze, defying all those who had dared to stare, he had prowled the limits of his humiliating cage with a heartbreaking dignity that had made her tender heart bleed.

'Are you hurt?' he asked in a dark, deep accented drawl that would have made her toes curl had she been able to feel them.

Slowly, carefully, she shook her head to express her continuing health. The fact that he was flattening her into a wet ditch was meaningless when she met those gorgeous eyes. She spread her visual net to appreciate the lush spiky black lashes that provided a fitting exotic frame for his deep-set gaze. He had a lean, hard-boned face that was angular and uncompromisingly male, yet possessed of such breathtaking intrinsic beauty that she could do nothing but stare.

Andreas looked down into the bluest eyes he had ever met. He was convinced they could not be naturally that bright turquoise colour and was equally suspicious of the spill of shiny pale blonde hair tumbling round her heart-shaped face like tangled silk. 'What the hell were you doing in the middle of the road?'

'Would you mind letting me up?' Hope mumbled apologetically.

With a stifled curse as he registered in rare embarrassment that he was still lying on top of the woman responsible for the death of his car, Andreas wrenched himself back from her. A faint tinge of colour demarcating his superb cheekbones as he questioned his own uncharacteristic loss of concentration, he sprang upright and reached down a lean, long-fingered hand to assist her. An unsought thought emerged out of nowhere: she had skin as smooth, soft and tempting as whipped cream.

'I wasn't in the middle of the road...I was scared you would drive on without seeing me,' Hope explained, wincing at the freezing chill of her clothing as she let him pull her upright. He was impossibly tall, so tall, she had to throw her head back on her shoulders to look up at him.

'You were standing in the centre of a very narrow road,' Andreas contradicted without hesitation. 'I had to swerve to avoid hitting you.'

Hope looked back down the road to where his car still smouldered. It was obvious even to her that when the last of the little flames died down, it would be a charred wreck fit only for the scrapyard. She could see that it had been a sports model of some kind and probably very expensive. That he appeared to be blaming her for the accident sent a current of guilty anxiety travelling through her.

'I'm really sorry about your car,' she said tautly, striving to sidestep the possibility of conflict. Having grown up in a family dominated by strong personalities, who had often been at loggerheads, she was accustomed to assuming the soothing role of a peacemaker.

Andreas surveyed the pathetic remains of his customised Ferrari, which he had only driven for the second time that day. He turned his arrogant dark head back to his companion and flicked his keen gaze over her at supersonic speed. He committed her every attribute to memory and dismissed her with every cold succeeding thought. Her clothes were drab and shabby. Of medium height, she was what his father would have called a healthy size and what any of his many female acquaintances who rejoiced in jutting bones would have called overweight. But no sooner had he reached that conclusion than he recalled how soft and feminine and sexy her full, ripe curves had felt under him and a startling spasm of pure, unvarnished lust arrowed through him at shattering speed.

'It's such a shame that you weren't able to avoid the tree,' Hope added, intending that as a sympathetic expression of regret.

'Avoiding *you* was my priority. Never mind the fact that, in the attempt, I could easily have killed myself,' Andreas countered with icy bite at what he interpreted as a veiled attack on his skill as a driver. Having dragged his attention from her, he had felt the heat of that startlingly inappropriate hunger subside as swiftly as it had arisen. He decided that the crash had temporarily deprived him of his wits and caused his libido to play a trick on his imagination: she had to be the least attractive woman he had ever met.

'But mercifully,' Hope bravely persisted in her efforts to offer comfort, 'we both have a lot to be grateful for—'

'Educate me on that score,' Andreas sliced back in an invitation that cracked like a whiplash.

'Sorry?' Hope prompted uncertainly, turquoise eyes locking to him in dismay.

'*Theos mou!* Explain exactly what you believe that I have to be grateful for at this moment in time,' Andreas demanded with derision, snowflakes beginning to encrust his cropped black hair as the fall grew heavier. 'I'm standing in a blizzard and I'm cold. It's getting dark. My favourite car has been obliterated from the face of the earth along with my mobile phone and I am stuck with a stranger.'

'But we're alive. Neither of us has been hurt,' Hope pointed out through chattering teeth, still keen as mustard to cheer him up.

He was stranded with Little Miss Sunshine, Andreas registered in disgust. 'May I make use of your mobile phone?'

'I'm sorry...I don't have one—'

'Then you must live nearby...how far is it to your home?' Andreas cut in, taking an impatient step forward.

'But I don't live round here,' she answered ruefully. 'I don't even know where I am.'

Ebony brows drawing together, Andreas frowned down at her as though she had confessed to something unbelievably stupid. 'How can that be?'

'I'm not a local,' Hope explained, trying to still a shiver and failing. 'I'm only in the area because I was attending an interview and I got a lift there. Then I started walking...I followed this signpost and I thought I couldn't be that far from the main road but I must have taken a wrong turn somewhere—'

'How long were you walking for?'

'A couple of hours and I haven't seen any houses for absolutely ages. That's why I didn't want you to drive past. I was getting a little concerned—'

Watching her shiver violently, Andreas noticed that her coat was dripping. 'When did you get wet?'

'There's a stream in that ditch,' she told him jerkily.

'How wet are you?'

Having established that she was soaked through to the skin, Andreas studied her with fulminating intensity, brilliant eyes flashing tawny. 'You should have said,' he censured. 'In sub-zero temperatures, you're liable to end up with hypothermia and I don't need the hassle.'

'I'm not going to be any hassle,' Hope swore hurriedly.

'I saw a barn a couple of fields back. You need shelter—'

'Really, I'll be fine. As soon as I start walking again, I'll warm up in no time,' Hope mumbled through fast-numbing lips, for of all things she hated to make the smallest nuisance of herself.

'You won't warm up until you get those clothes off,' Andreas asserted, planting a managing arm to her spine to urge her along at a pace faster than was comfortable for her much shorter legs.

Her lips were too numb for her to laugh at the very idea of getting her clothes off in the presence of a strange man. But she was tickled pink by his instant response to what he saw as an emergency. In a flash, he had abandoned all lament about his wrecked car and his own lack of comfort to put her needs first. At a similar speed he had found a solution to the problem and he was taking charge.

Wasn't that supposed to be a typically male response? Only it was not a response that was as common as popular report liked to suggest, Hope reflected thoughtfully. Neither her father nor her brother had been the least bit tempted to help her out by solving problems. In fact both the men in her life had beat a very fast retreat from the demands placed on them by her mother's long illness. She had been forced to accept that neither man was strong enough to cope with that challenge and that, as she *was* capable, there was no point blaming them for their weakness.

'What's your name?' she asked him. 'I'm Hope... Hope Evans.'

'Andreas,' Andreas delivered grimly, watching her attempt to climb a farm gate with incredulous eyes. With purposeful hands he lifted her down from her wobbly perch on the second bar so that he could unlatch the gate for their entry.

'Oh, thanks...' Wretched with cold as she was, Hope was breathless at having received that amount of attention and shaken that he had managed to lift her without apparent effort. But then she could not recall anyone trying to lift her after the age of ten. She would never forget, however, the cruel taunts she had earned at school for the generous bodily proportions that had been the exact opposite of the fashionable slenderness possessed by the most popular girls in her form.

As she lurched into a ditch by the hedge where the snow was lying in a dangerously deceptive drift Andreas hauled her back to his side. 'Watch where you walk...'

The numbness of her feet was making it well nigh impossible for her to judge where her steps fell. The natural stone building ahead seemed reassuringly close, however, and she tried to push herself on but stumbled again. Expelling his breath in an impatient hiss, Andreas bent down and lifted her up into his arms to trudge the last few yards.

Instantly, Hope exploded into embarrassed speech. 'Put me down, for goodness' sake...you'll strain yourself! I'm far too heavy—'

'You're not and if you fall, you could easily break a limb,' Andreas pointed out.

'And you don't want the hassle,' Hope completed in a small voice as he lowered her to the beaten earth floor towards the back of the dim barn, which was open to the elements on the side closest to the road.

Before she could even guess what he was doing, Andreas tugged off her coat. Her suit jacket peeled off with it. 'My goodness!' she gasped, lurching back a step from him in consternation.

'When you get the rest off, you can use my coat for cover,' Andreas declared, shrugging broad shoulders free of the heavy wool overcoat and extending it with decisive hands.

Hot pink embarrassment washed colour to the roots of Hope's hair. Grasping the coat with reluctance, she hovered. She was too practical to continue questioning his assertion that she had to take off her sodden clothing.

'I'll get on with lighting a fire so that you can warm up,' Andreas pronounced, planning that he would then leave her ensconced while he sought out a house and a phone. He would get there a hell of a lot faster on his own.

There was a massive woodpile stacked against the wall. She stepped to the far side of it, rested his coat over the protruding logs and began with chilled hands to clumsily undress. Removing her trousers was a dreadful struggle because her fingers were numb and the fabric clung to her wet skin. She pulled off her heavy sweater with equal difficulty and then, shivering violently and clad only in a damp bra, panties and ankle boots, she dug her arms into his overcoat. The coat drowned her, reaching down to her ankles, hanging off her shoulders and masking her hands as though she were a child dressing up in adult clothes. The silk lining made her shiver but the very weight of the wool garment bore the promise of greater warmth. Wrapped in the capacious depths of his carefully buttoned coat, she crept back into view.

Andreas was industriously engaged in piling up small pieces of kindling wood with some larger chunks of fuel already stacked in readiness. Again she was impressed by the quiet speed and efficiency with which he got things done. He was resourceful. He didn't make a fuss. He didn't agonise over decisions and he didn't moan and whinge about the necessity either: he just did the job. She had definitely picked a winner to get stranded with in the snow.

She studied him, admiring the trendy cut of his luxuriant black hair, the sleek, smooth and undoubtedly very expensive tailoring of the charcoal-grey suit he wore teamed with a dark shirt and a silk tie. He looked like a high-flying business executive, a real urban sophisticate, the sort of guy she would have been too afraid even to speak to in normal circumstances.

'One small problem...I don't smoke,' he murmured.

'Oh...I can help there,' Hope recalled, hurriedly digging into her handbag and producing a cheap plastic lighter. 'I don't smoke either but I thought my future employer might and I didn't want to seem disapproving.'

As he waited for her to complete that rather intriguing explanation Andreas glanced up and registered in surprise that she was very far from being the least attractive woman he had ever met. In the dim interior, her pale blonde hair, now loose and falling almost to her shoulders, glowed like silver against the black upraised collar of his coat. Her cheeks were flushed, her eyes bright. She was smiling at him and when she smiled, her whole face lit up. Lost in the depths of his coat, she looked startlingly appealing.

'Here...' Hope extended the lighter.

'*Efharisto...*' Andreas thanked her gravely, mentally querying her unexpected pull for him. She was blonde and rather short and he went for tall, leggy brunettes.

'*Parakalo*…you're welcome,' Hope responded with a weak grin, striving to move her feet to instil a little feeling back into her toes. 'So, you're Greek?'

'Yes.' Protecting the minuscule blaze of wood shavings from the wind whistling through the cracks in the wall, Andreas fed the fire. She was virtually naked below his coat. It was that knowledge that was making her appear appealing to him, he told himself in exasperation. He resisted a foolish urge to look at her again. Why would he even *want* to look at her again?

'I love Greece…well, I've only been there once but it was really beautiful.' When her companion failed to grab that conversational opener, Hope added, 'You're used to lighting fires, aren't you?'

'No, as it happens,' Andreas remarked, dry as dust. 'But I don't need to be the equivalent of a rocket scientist to create a blaze.'

Hope reddened. 'I'm talking too much.'

Andreas told himself that he was glad that she had taken the hint. Yet when he looked up and saw the stoic look of accepting hurt in her face, he felt as though someone had kicked him hard in the stomach. When had he become so rude and insensitive?

'No. I'm a man of few words and you're good company,' he assured her.

She gave him a huge surprised smile and, blushing like a schoolgirl, she threaded her hands inside the sleeves of his over-large coat and shuffled her feet. 'Honestly?'

'Honestly,' Andreas murmured, taken aback by her

response to the mildest of compliments and involuntarily touched.

He coaxed the fire into slow life. She was so cold she was shivering without even being aware of it. As the fire crackled he sprang up to his full height of six feet four and approached her. 'There's a hip flask in the left pocket of my coat.'

Hope reached in and lifted it out.

'Take a drink before you freeze.'

'I'm not used to it...I couldn't—'

Andreas groaned out loud. Taking the flask from her, he opened it. 'Be sensible.'

Hope sipped and then grew bolder. When the alcohol raced like a leaping flame down her throat she choked, coughing and spluttering.

Closing the flask for her, Andreas surveyed her and rueful amusement tilted his wide, sensual mouth. 'You weren't joking when you said you weren't used to it.'

Hope sucked in a jerky breath and wrapped her arms round herself. 'I didn't know I could feel this cold,' she confided in a rush.

Andreas uncrossed her arms, closed lean, strong hands over hers and slowly drew her close. 'Think of me as a hot blanket,' he urged.

Her lashes fluttered in confusion. 'I don't think I could...'

'Try. It will be a while before the fire puts out enough heat to defrost you.'

Hope lifted wide eyes as turquoise as the Aegean Sea on a summer day. 'I suppose...' she mumbled.

'Do you wear coloured contact lenses?' Andreas enquired, black brows pleating because even as he spoke he questioned the inanity of his enquiry.

'You must be joking... I can't even afford make-up!' Hope's state of nerves was betrayed by the tiny jerk she gave as he eased her into physical connection with his tall, well-built body. All of a sudden her heart felt as if it were jumping inside her chest and she could hardly catch her breath.

'You have perfect skin...you don't need it,' Andreas said thickly, his big, powerful body growing rigid. Even the separation of their clothing could not dull his high-voltage awareness of the tantalising softness of her lush, feminine curves. In spite of his every effort to freeze his own all-too-male reactions, his libido was rocketing into overdrive.

That close he turned her bones to jelly and Hope couldn't think straight. She looked up and connected with his mesmerising dark golden eyes. A dulled heaviness gripped her lower limbs while a tight, hard knot of agonising tension formed in her pelvis. He lowered his handsome dark head and she guessed what was going to happen before it happened but still couldn't believe that he would actually do it.

But Andreas confounded her expectations and captured her mouth with hungry urgency. That single kiss devastated her and as it began, it continued, his tongue delving between her readily parted lips to demand greater intimacy. She was defenceless against that wild, sweet tide of sensation, for her body flared into sudden desperate life. The tense knot low in her stomach spiralled into a drugging flare of heat that suffused her entire body with explosive effect. Only the need to breathe conquered that wicked heat and she had to pull her swollen lips free to drag in a great gulp of oxygen.

Andreas gazed down at her with heavily lidded

dark eyes and then, abruptly, he yanked his head up and colour delineated his hard cheekbones. '*Theos mou*…I had no intention of…' His handsome mouth clenched. 'I should never have touched you. I'm sorry.'

'Are you married?' Hope demanded, voicing her worst fear instantaneously and only contriving to drag her hands from him as she finished speaking.

'No.'

'Engaged?' Hope was no longer cold. Her entire body felt as though it were hot as a furnace with embarrassment.

His ebony brows pleated. 'No.'

'Then there's no need to apologise,' Hope declared half under her breath, scrupulously avoiding his scrutiny while she struggled to get a grip on herself. The way he had made her feel had been a revelation to her and she felt incredibly vulnerable and confused. Her fingers clenched into the cuffs of the coat sleeves to prevent her hands from reaching back to him. She turned away in an awkward semi-circle, so many thoughts and emotions and physical feelings bombarding her that she felt momentarily overwhelmed.

Her first real kiss and he had apologised. It would be terribly uncool to confess that he had thrilled the socks off her and that if he wanted to do it again he was more than welcome. Her face flamed with guilt and bewilderment. For goodness' sake, where had that shameless thought come from? With hands that trembled she made herself concentrate long enough to pick up and drape her wet clothing over the pile of logs.

'I've upset you,' Andreas breathed.

Hope whirled round, turquoise eyes bright as pre-

cious stones in her flushed heart-shaped face. 'No...
I'm not upset.'

She felt a hundred things but not upset: shocked,
bemused and exhilarated by the sheer strength of her
response to him. For too many years she had lived in
a world empty of any form of excitement. Andreas
was the most exciting thing that had ever happened
to her and so great was her fascination that it hurt to
deny herself the pleasure of looking at him.

'I planned to leave you here alone,' Andreas
drawled flatly, still struggling to get a handle on his
own inexplicable behaviour and somewhat stunned by
his loss of control.

Startled, Hope whirled round. 'Why? Where were
you planning to go?'

'I intended to try and find a house but it's too dark
now.'

'And I have your coat. Much better to wait until
daylight.' Hope snatched in a stark breath of the icy
air while she gazed out at the fast-swirling snow being
blown about by the wind. It was no longer possible
to see even the hedges bounding the road.

She drew nearer to the fire and then knelt down
beside it to take advantage of the heat the flames were
beginning to generate.

'Tell me about your interview,' Andreas invited,
having noted that she would no longer meet his gaze
and determined to eradicate her unease. 'What was
the job?'

'The position of live-in companion to an elderly
woman but the interview never happened,' Hope confided ruefully. 'When I got to the house I found out
that a relative had moved in with the lady instead and
there was no longer a job available.'

'So these people didn't bother to cancel your interview and left you stranded?' Andreas queried with disapproval.

'I asked why I hadn't been contacted but the woman who spoke to me said it was nothing to do with her because she hadn't placed the ad in the first place.' Hope just shrugged and smiled wryly. 'That's life.'

'You are far too forgiving,' Andreas told her. 'Why did you want work of that nature?'

'I'm not qualified for anything else...at least, not at present.' Hope wanted a stable roof over her head and a period of steady employment before she checked out what she considered to be the much more remote and ambitious possibility of winning a place on a design course. 'I also need somewhere to live and it would've suited me very well. Where were you travelling?'

'I was heading back to London.'

'Why did you kiss me?'

It was hard to know which of them was most surprised by that very abrupt question: Hope, who had not known that she was about to embarrass herself by asking for clarification on that score, or Andreas, who had never been faced with such a bald demand to know his motivation before.

Dark golden eyes surveyed her steadily. 'Why do you think?'

Face hot again, Hope studied her tightly linked hands. 'I haven't a clue...I was just curious.'

'You're very sexy.'

Her lashes swept up on her astonished gaze. 'Are you serious?'

'I should know...I'm a connoisseur,' Andreas asserted without hesitation.

Her lush, full mouth curved into a grin, for she liked his frankness. So, he liked women and no doubt in large numbers. And why should he not? He was gorgeous and women had to fall for him in droves. Naturally he took advantage and who could blame him? If deep down a little twinge of pain stabbed at her that that should be so, she ignored it.

After all, she was much more interested in what Andreas had said prior to that final statement. It seemed like a miracle to her but he had called her sexy. Hope was used to thinking of herself as plain, overweight and ordinary. She had spent years hating her own body and longing to be thinner. To that end she had dieted and exercised and her weight had fluctuated up and down while the slender figure she craved continued to elude her. Even the mother she loved had sighed over her daughter's lack of looks and lamented her keen appetite.

Yet Andreas, who was heartbreakingly handsome, considered her attractive. And not only that...he thought she was sexy. Even better he had proven his own conviction by succumbing to charms she had not known she had. She reckoned that she was probably going to love him until the day she died for allowing her to feel just once like a young and pretty woman. She had waited what felt like half a lifetime to hear such words and had truly believed that she would die without ever hearing them. He was the fulfilment of a dream and she studied him with massive and grateful concentration.

'So what do you do for a living?' Hope asked chattily.

'I deal with investments.'

'I suppose you're stuck at a desk all the time studying figures and it's a bit boring. Still, somebody has to do it.' Her turquoise eyes were warm with sympathy.

Andreas got a high out of his immensely successful career but he had met far too many women who faked an interest in finance in an effort to impress him. Hope, he recognised, was not tempted in that direction. His rare smile illuminated his lean bronzed features, which in repose could seem grave and cold.

'Would you like some chocolate?' she asked, rooting round in her capacious bag and emerging with a giant bar and only then seeing that smile and riveted by it. He had buckets of charisma and she was entrapped.

'Yes…before you melt it,' Andreas laughed, hunkering down to reach for the bar, which she was holding perilously close to the fire. He broke off a piece and let his brilliant gaze sweep from her clear bright eyes and the fascination she couldn't hide to the ripe curve of her lips. He remembered the intoxicating taste of her and the laughter left him to be replaced by a disturbingly strong desire to haul her back into his arms. He put the square of chocolate he had intended for himself into her mouth instead.

'Oh…' Hope gasped in surprise and closed her eyes in slow, blissful appreciation as the cold chocolate began melting against her tongue.

Andreas was transfixed by the expression she wore. He could not take his attention from her. He wondered if she would react like that to him in bed. He tried to kill the thought. He tried to suppress the powerful tide of hunger she ignited in him, but his usually disciplined libido was behaving like a runaway train.

Her lashes lifted. 'I would do just about anything for chocolate…'

Her voice faded away and her mouth ran dry on the glittering blaze she met in his intent golden eyes. On a level of understanding she had not even known she possessed she recognised his hunger and she leant forward without even thinking about what she was doing and sought his hard, sensual mouth again for herself. With a hungry growl, Andreas came down on his knees and kissed her until the blood drummed at an insane rate through her veins and her head swam.

'I'll buy you chocolate every day,' Andreas promised huskily.

'You know…I wasn't meaning anything provocative,' Hope warned him anxiously.

'I know.' Long fingers framed her cheekbones while his eyes devoured her. 'I find that straightforward streak of yours very refreshing.'

'Other people call me blunt—'

'Whatever, I don't meet with much of it,' Andreas admitted thickly, his hands not quite steady on her. 'I also want you so much it hurts to deny myself. That's a first for me.'

Hope felt utterly unlike herself. It was as though at that first kiss she had become an alien inside her own once familiar skin. She felt wild and greedy and joyous and as tempting as Cleopatra. All the years of stoically repressed regret at the manner in which life was passing her by, all the wistful longings and fanciful dreams that crowded out the fertile imagination she hid behind a front of no-nonsense practicality finally got to break free. Andreas was the embodiment of her every fantasy.

'A first for me too,' she confided breathlessly.

He unbuttoned the coat and then froze, a rare glint of confusion in the wondering appraisal he gave her. He had no grasp of quite how the situation had developed but he couldn't make himself let go of her. 'We have to be out of our minds—'

Hope closed her fingers into the lapels of his suit jacket. 'Shush…don't spoil it,' she whispered pleadingly.

Andreas spread her back against his coat and let his mouth glide down the length of her throat. 'Tell me when to stop…'

With no intention of calling a halt at any point, Hope shivered with delicious tension and lay there. She booted the misgivings struggling to be heard out of her mind and slammed shut the door on them for good measure. For twenty-eight years she had been good and just once, and for the space of one stolen, secret night, she was going to be bad and what was more she was going to enjoy it.

He unsnapped the lace bra and groaned out loud at the creamy swell of her pouting breasts in the firelight. 'You have a body to die for.'

Hot with a mix of self-consciousness and helpless longing, she opened her eyes to see if he was teasing: his appreciation spoke for him. With reverent hands he toyed with the tender pink peaks already straining into thrusting points. Deep down inside she felt as if she were burning and her hips shifted in a pointless effort to contain the feeling. Within very little time the whole world centred on him and what he was doing to her.

He employed his knowing mouth on the stiff crests that crowned her breasts and the inner thrum of her body's response became so powerful she could not stay still. Her entire skin surface felt unbearably sensitive but more than anything she was aware of the damp ache at the swollen heart of her.

'Andreas…' She sounded his name in a throaty, pleading purr and at last he touched her where she most needed to be touched.

Sensation electrified her and took her to a place she had never been before, where all that mattered was the sensual glory of his touch and the wildness that was being born within her. She writhed, wrapped herself round him, lost in the hot, male scent of his skin and hair and the enervating roughness of his hard, muscular body against her.

'I can't wait…' Andreas confessed rawly, passion breaking through his formidable control at a level of excitement he had never known before.

The sheer overload of physical pleasure had driven her to a tortured peak and she was helpless in the hold of the powerful craving that controlled her. He pulled her under him and she was with him every step of the way. With an earthy groan he sank into the slick, hot heat of her and met with unexpected resistance.

'You're a virgin?' he breathed in stark shock.

'Don't stop…' she gasped, reaching up to lock imprisoning arms round him.

He yielded and swept her through the sharp little pain into a fast, frantic rhythm as primal as the overpowering sensations that had taken her over. Intolerable excitement pushed her into ecstasy and a cocoon of pleasure. In the aftermath, she felt amazingly silly and happy and buoyant.

Andreas gazed at Hope with wondering golden eyes and then he gathered her very carefully back into the warmth of his coat and tugged her into his arms. He kissed her brow. 'You're very sweet...but you should have told me I'd be the first.'

'It was my business,' Hope muttered, burying her face into his shoulder, fighting off the shock of what she had just done.

'But now's it mine,' Andreas asserted, determined fingers tipping her chin up so that he could look at her again in the flickering light cast by the burning logs. 'I think that in the very near future you will decide to move to London and I will be your lover.'

'Why would I do that?' Hope dared to ask although sparkles of joy were running through her like precious gold dust.

His hard, sensual mouth slashed into a sudden smile of breathtaking assurance. 'Because I will ask you to and you won't be able to resist.'

Her heart was bouncing like a rubber ball inside her chest and she smiled up at him with all the natural warmth that was the very core of her character.

CHAPTER ONE

ALMOST two years later, Hope sat in a fashionable London café waiting for her friend Vanessa's arrival.

Her thoughts were miles away and centred entirely on Andreas. She was dreamily wondering how she could best celebrate the second anniversary of that first eventful meeting. By seeking out a snow-bound barn? That would not be a good idea, she conceded with a grin. Andreas disliked inconvenience, cold and, indeed, had a very low tolerance threshold for any form of discomfort.

'Sorry I'm late.' A slim redhead with sharp but attractive features and bright brown eyes sank down into the seat opposite and settled a heavy camera case down. 'If that hair of yours grows any longer,' she remarked, surveying the pale blonde hair Hope wore secured at her nape but which reached halfway to her waist, 'people are going to start wondering if you've got Rapunzel fantasies.'

Hope blinked. 'I beg your pardon?'

'You know...the lady in the fairy tale who got locked up in the tower and let her long hair down to be used as a ladder to rescue her,' Vanessa clarified. 'Only unfortunately for her, it wasn't the handsome prince who climbed up, it was the witch. Be warned.'

Hope laughed and they ordered coffee. She was accustomed to her more sophisticated friend's cynical outlook on life. The daughter of a famous artist, Vanessa had survived a Bohemian and unstable childhood to become a gifted photographer. But the red-head still bore the scars inflicted by parents who had enjoyed tempestuous love lives.

'So, how is *your* handsome prince?' Vanessa enquired a tinge dryly.

Hope was impervious to that tone and her eyes sparkled. 'Andreas is great. Very busy, of course, but he phones me a lot when he's out of the country—'

'A mobile phone being Andreas's equivalent of a ball and chain,' her friend mocked. 'I seem to recall that if you switch it off he wants an explanation in triplicate.'

'He just likes to know where I am. He worries about me,' Hope countered equably. 'Do you realise that in ten days' time, Andreas and I will have been together for two whole years?'

'Wow. The guy who doesn't commit is going for gold. You could be making gossip column headlines. Of course,' Vanessa murmured wryly, 'the world would first have to know you existed and you remain a very well-kept secret.'

'Andreas hates media attention and he knows I wouldn't like it either. I'm a very contented secret,' Hope admitted, telling herself with the ease of long habit that what little time she had with Andreas would be very much diluted if she had to share him with a social whirl and lots of people as well. 'Right now, I'm trying to think of some special way to celebrate our anniversary.'

'Andreas didn't make the effort to mark the occasion last year, did he?'

'I doubt if it even occurred to him that we had been together an entire year. I shouldn't have sat around waiting for *him* to say or do something, I should just have reminded him,' Hope said ruefully

'Did he ever mention it afterwards?'

Hope shook her head.

'Then, let me offer you a piece of advice,' the younger woman remarked. 'If you want to hang onto Andreas Nicolaidis, resist the urge to celebrate your second anniversary in his presence.'

'But why?'

'The reminder that you've been around for two years might set the cold wind of change blowing.'

'What are you trying to say to me?' Hope prompted anxiously.

Vanessa compressed her lips and sighed. 'I just feel you're wasting your time with Andreas. He didn't even bother to show up the night you collected the top award for your design course.'

'His flight was delayed.'

'Was it?' The younger woman looked unimpressed. 'He has no interest in anything in your life unless it directly affects him.'

'Andreas isn't artistic…or into fashion. I don't expect him to take an interest in the handbags I design—'

'He hasn't introduced you to a single member of his family or to any of his friends. If he takes you out it's to some place where he won't be bothered by the paparazzi and where he won't be seen with you. He's kept his life separate from yours and he keeps you in a little restricted box. Why don't you face facts? You're his mistress in everything but name—'

'That's not true! Andreas doesn't keep me. I take nothing from him…OK, I live in that flat, but I pay all my own expenses and I don't accept expensive gifts or anything from him,' Hope reasoned in a low-pitched tone of urgency.

'But it's not a question of what *you* think, it's all about what Andreas thinks and how he treats you—'

'He cares about me...he treats me really well,' Hope argued tightly.

Vanessa gave her a concerned look but Hope felt far too raw to take comfort from a sympathy that could only further dent her pride. 'Why shouldn't he? You're devoted to him and he knows it and he uses it. He set the boundaries of your relationship way back at the beginning—'

'No...there were no rules set. I am not his mistress...I wouldn't *be* his mistress!' Hope stated in an almost fierce undertone.

'So he was too smooth an operator to put a label on it. Has he ever mentioned a future with you? Love? Marriage? Children?'

Battered down by those bold words, Hope almost flinched.

'You have a right to ask where things are going at any stage of a relationship,' Vanessa informed her and then she changed the subject.

Afterwards, Hope had no real idea what she had discussed with Vanessa beyond that point. She remembered having smiled a lot. She had been keen to reassure her closest friend that she was not offended by that blunt appraisal of her relationship with Andreas. But, in truth, those same comments had blown her peace of mind sky-high and caused her considerable pain. Vanessa's every word replayed again and again in Hope's troubled thoughts. She was devastated when she was forced to acknowledge that most of what the other woman had said had been based on unarguable fact rather than personal opinion.

Only hours earlier, Hope had felt supremely happy and perfectly contented with her life and with Andreas's central position within it. It had been Vanessa who had sowed discontent inside her. Yet she did not blame her friend. After all, Vanessa had only shown her a more disturbing interpretation of limitations that Hope had simply accepted. Slowly and painfully, Hope felt all the concerns that she had suppressed and all the questions she had never dared to ask Andreas rise like taunts to the surface of her mind.

Andreas had never taken her to Greece, although he knew that she longed to visit the country of his birth with him. Even though his one and only sibling, his younger sister, Elyssa, was married to an Englishman and lived in London, Andreas had not succumbed to Hope's gentle hints that she would like to meet Elyssa. Hope had always avoided dwelling on that omission and had told herself that in time Andreas would make that suggestion on his own account. In the same way, she had also convinced herself that she was unconcerned by her lack of contact with Andreas's family and friends. But he had never given her the option, had he?

It was equally true that Andreas had never been known to make a reference to the future as something they might share...at least not a future that extended further than a calendar month ahead in his highly organised schedule. Not once had he mentioned marriage or a desire for children. As for love, well, he was prone to making cutting comments on that topic and she had learned to avoid the subject.

Her eyes stung with a surge of rare tears as she entered the big penthouse apartment that had become her home. Andreas might be in no hurry to offer commitment, but that still did not mean that she was his mistress. *Did it?* By nature, Andreas was reserved and cautious. Another doubt crept in to make itself heard: how could she even tell herself that they lived together? In the strictest sense they did not because Andreas continued to own and make occasional use of another, even more substantial city property. He had pointed out that the apartment was a necessary convenience for him because it was a lot closer to his office than his town house. His relatives also stayed at the town house when they visited London, as did he when it suited him. Furthermore, Hope had never set foot inside the town house...

Suddenly, Hope was seeing the foundations of her happiness wash away like sand on a beach. She adored Andreas. She had truly believed that their relationship was wonderful and well worth cherishing. But Vanessa's frankly offered opinion had lacerated Hope's pride and destroyed her confidence. Was it possible that she had been wilfully blind rather than face the harsh, hurtful truth? Was it possible that, like the penthouse apartment, she was really just a convenience to Andreas too? A sexual rather than residential convenience?

The phone in the echoing reception hall was ringing. After a moment of hesitation, she picked up.

'Why has your mobile been switched off for three hours?' Andreas demanded. 'Where have you been?'

'I was meeting Vanessa and...er...shopping and I forgot to put it on again.' Hope crossed two sets of fingers as she told that small lie and swallowed hard.

'I'll be with you by eight tomorrow night. So, talk to me,' Andreas invited, because he had taken a break for coffee and he could always depend on her to fill the space with the minutiae of her daily existence. No matter where he was in the world, he could pick up the phone and within minutes her tide of chirpy chatter would filter away all stress and entertain him. Hope had been very well named. She never said anything bad about anyone. She went out of her way to do favours for total strangers. She put a positive spin on every experience.

Her mind was blank. 'What about?'

'Anything and everything…how clothes are shrinking in size to fuel the diet industry…the addictive quality of chocolate…what a lovely day it is…how even wet days can be fun…what wonderfully pleasant people you have met in the apartment foyer, on the street, in the stores,' Andreas enumerated without hesitation. 'I'm used to a deluge of irrepressibly cheerful chatter.'

Hope's face flamed. Did he see her as a mindless babbler? What *did* he see in her? She had always wondered. It took huge effort but she managed to talk and it must have been mindless because, the whole time, one half of her was concentrated on the less-than-encouraging reflection she could see in the contemporary mirror on the wall opposite. How could any guy who looked like Andreas really care for a woman her shape and size? Stop it, stop it, *stop it*, the voice of common sense urged her. With resolute courage, she turned away from the mirror and assured herself that self-doubt was not about to make her bolt to the kitchen and use food as a source of comfort.

In Switzerland, Andreas set down his phone, a

frown dividing his ebony brows as his analytical brain homed in on the question of what had upset Hope. She was not prone to moods. Indeed her temperament was remarkably even and upbeat. When something bothered her, she shared it with him. In fact, she told him immediately and appreciated his advice. What kind of problem would she choose not to share with him?

Although she remained blissfully unaware of the fact, Hope was currently enjoying very discreet twenty-four-hour protection. Andreas, in common with many wealthy individuals, had suffered threats. Concerned that Hope might also be targeted, Andreas had hired security professionals to watch over her. Initially he had planned to tell her. But he had feared that the safeguards he had put in place might frighten her. She was friendly and trusting and thought the very best of everyone she met. He did not want that to change and had decided that it was kinder to leave her in ignorance. Only for an instant did he consider contacting her security team to find out where she had been and whom she had been with. That would be taking advantage of the situation and he respected her privacy. Even so, a sense of annoyance that Hope should for once have given him cause for disquiet made Andreas icy cold and tough with the executives who at his signal returned to the conference table.

Hope always dressed up for Andreas. Staring into her wardrobe, she was mentally dividing it into three separate collections of clothes. Of the three, usually only one set fitted her at any one time. The first had enjoyed a brief but glittering life after a crash diet and the second was filled with all the replacement clothes in different sizes that she had had to buy while she'd steadily regained the weight she had lost. The third was full of stalwart outfits with forgivingly stretchy proportions. Almost everything was bright in colour. As she yanked out a dress her head spun a little and she felt momentarily dizzy enough to sink down on the edge of the bed. It had not been the first time that she had felt that way in recent weeks but she reckoned that the light-headed feeling was an irritating hangover from a virus she had found hard to shake off during the autumn. No doubt the bug was still working its slow way out of her system and she would be wasting her doctor's time if she approached her with such a vague symptom.

In an hour, Andreas would be with her again and excitement was leaping through Hope in intoxicating waves. She refused to torment herself with Vanessa's gloomy forecast of doom and disappointment. Her friend had only wanted to put her on her guard, had in short spoken up out of pure, disinterested kindness. But Hope was equally well aware that Vanessa, who had had several unfortunate experiences, cherished a pronounced distrust of men and their motives. Furthermore, Vanessa had never met Andreas, had not even had the opportunity to appreciate what a wonderful guy he was.

Andreas kept the media at arm's length and suffered accordingly for his determination to protect his privacy. It took a great deal to anger Hope but she had been very much annoyed by several magazine articles and newspaper columns that had utilised old photos and old stories to enable their continued unjust depiction of Andreas as a ruthless, callous womaniser who was merciless in business. Had Vanessa read those items and been influenced by them?

As Hope brushed her hair she was thinking about the male she knew. Strong, generous, wildly passionate, literally everything she wanted in a man wrapped up in one fantastic package. Even though Andreas hated roughing it, he took her on picnics because he knew she loved them. Sightseeing bored him to death but he had flown her out to Paris, Rome and a host of other fabulous cities so that she could explore her passion for history in his company. Whenever she had been scared, discouraged or in need of support, he had been there for her. She loved him with her whole heart and soul for a host of very understandable reasons. On the debit side…? No, no, she wasn't going there, she was determined not to allow foolish negativity to creep in and wreak havoc with her happiness.

Andreas called her from the airport.

'I'm counting the minutes,' she told him truthfully.

He called her from the limo when it got stuck in city traffic.

'I can't bear it…' she gasped strickenly.

'Have you any idea how much I've missed you?' Andreas finally broke through his cool to demand in his final call made as he stepped into the lift to come up to the apartment.

By that stage, Hope was in a heady fever of anticipation. The front door opened: she saw him and all intelligent thought ceased. Her knees felt weak. She leant back against the wall to steady herself. Everything about Andreas thrilled her to death. From the stubborn angle of his proud dark head to the lithe, leashed power and grace of his hard, muscular frame, he was spectacularly male. Lamplight burnished his cropped black hair and cast his lean, bronzed features into tantalising angles of light and shade. He was breathtakingly handsome and he still only had to walk through the door to make her heart threaten cardiac arrest.

Andreas kicked the door shut behind him and powered on across the hall to haul her into his arms. For an endless moment of bliss she was lost in the glorious touch and feel of him. Her nostrils flared on the familiar male scent of his skin overlaid with a faint tang of designer lotion and her responses went into overdrive. 'Andreas...' she breathed unsteadily.

'If you could travel with me, we would have more time together.' Brilliant dark golden eyes entrapped her misty gaze, his accented drawl husky and reasonable in tone, for he chose his moments with care. 'Think about that. You could let your artistic endeavours take a back seat for a while.'

And lose her independence, which was quite out of the question, Hope acknowledged while she agonised with guilty longing over the seductive idea of being able to see more of Andreas. 'I couldn't...'

His hands closing over her smaller ones, and content to have planted yet another seed, Andreas pinned her back against the wall with all the single-minded purpose of a male guided by lustful intent. She succumbed to the allure of his hard, sensual mouth with the same fervour she would have employed in a life-or-death situation. He tasted like heaven, like something addictive she could not do without, and she clung. The tight knot of excitement in her belly fired her every nerve ending into an eager blaze of expectation. He dropped her hands to curve possessive fin-

gers to the full, feminine swell of her hips and lift her
into stirring connection with his bold erection.

'Oh…' she moaned, melting like honey in sunlight
while the wicked throb of helpless hunger shimmied
down into her pelvis and made her ache.

Plastered to every line of his big, powerful frame,
she dragged her mouth free to snatch in a necessary
gulp of oxygen while dimly her mind prompted her
to recall an important ritual that she could not afford
to overlook. 'Your mobile…' she gasped.

Andreas tensed.

'It's me or the phone,' Hope reminded him reluc-
tantly.

One-handed, Andreas wrenched the phone from his
jacket, switched it off and tossed it down on the hall-
stand. He returned to plundering her mouth with devouring hunger and then wrenched himself back from
her, dark colour scoring his aristocratic cheekbones.
'For once, we are going to be cool and make it out
of the hall.'

Dazed by passion, Hope slowly nodded.

With determination Andreas angled her away from
the wall and backed her towards the bedroom. 'If I
surrender my phone, you have to make it worth my
while, *pedhi mou.*'

'Oh…' Hope gazed back at him, soft mouth pink
and tingling from the heat of his, her legs unsteady
supports. The blaze of sexual challenge in his eyes
imprisoned her as surely as a chain. A blinding wave
of excitement sizzled through her.

Andreas surveyed her with scorching satisfaction.
He ran down the zip on her turquoise dress and shimmied it down over her hips to expose the pink lace
bra and panties that moulded her ripe curves. He

vented a husky masculine sound of appreciation.
'You're superb...'

Self-conscious colour flushed her cheeks and even
burnished the slope of her full breasts. Scooping her
up, he deposited her on the bed, his rare charismatic
smile flashing across his lean dark features, and her
heart leapt as though it had a life of its own.

'Don't move,' he told her with urgency.

'I'm not going anywhere,' she whispered, her attention locked to him like a magnet as he peeled off
the tailored jacket of his business suit.

He looked sensational. Lithe, dark and arrestingly
handsome, he emanated the prowling, lethal sexiness
of a predator. Butterflies were fluttering in her tummy
and she was on a helpless high of anticipation. But
on another level, she suddenly discovered that she
was fighting off a sense of shame that she should be
lying on a bed in her underwear for his benefit. She
had not been raised in a liberal home and when
Andreas had come into her life she had not just
thrown away the rulebook, she had virtually burned
it. Did she mean anything to him? Or was what they
had just a casual thing on his terms?

'Do you think about me when you're away?' Hope
blurted out.

His shirt hanging loose on his bronzed muscular
chest, Andreas came down on the bed and laughed
out loud. 'After two weeks without sex?' he teased in
his dark deep drawl. 'By this week, I was thinking
about you at least once a minute!'

Hope flushed to the roots of her pale hair, hurt and
disappointment scything through her that he should
be so literal. 'That wasn't what I meant.'

Andreas hauled her up against him with strong

hands, and golden eyes ablaze with arrogant confidence assailed hers. 'Don't ask a Greek trick questions,' he warned her. 'You're my lover. Of course I think about you.'

Without hesitation, he plundered her mouth and her uneasy thoughts blurred. Fire sparked low in her belly and a wave of tormenting hunger consumed her. Two weeks without Andreas felt like half a lifetime. Even as she doubted his commitment, she could not resist her need to take refuge in his passion. Her body was taut with sensitivity, begging for sensation. The expert caress of his hands on her breasts made her moan. The rosy buds crowning her tender flesh tingled and when he utilised his teeth and his tongue on those inflamed peaks, she writhed, control slipping from her as steadily as any form of rational awareness.

Her heart was racing, the breath catching in her dry throat. He was pure bronzed elemental male and he knew exactly what inflamed her. He found the hot, swollen secret at the heart of her and clever fingers drove her to ever more desperate heights of longing. The passion took over, roaring through her twisting, turning length like an explosive fireball.

'This is how I like to picture you,' Andreas rasped with raw satisfaction. 'Out of your mind with the pleasure I give you.'

He sank into her with ravishing force and her body leapt and clenched. The frenzy of excitement mastered her with terrifying immediacy. Delirious with desire, she was way beyond any hope of mastering the tempestuous surge of her responses. Her need for Andreas was almost painfully intense. His passion pushed her to a wild peak of unbearable pleasure and then she fell down and down and down into a state of turbulence that bore no resemblance to her usual languorous sense of peace and happiness. Her body was satisfied but her emotions were raw. Tears lashed her eyes and overflowed before she even knew what was happening to her.

Andreas rolled over onto his back. In the act of rearranging her on top of him, he pushed her hair gently off her face and his fingers lingered on her damp cheekbone. 'What's wrong?' he demanded.

'Nothing's wrong.' Hope gulped. 'I don't know why I'm crying. It's silly.'

Foreboding nudged at Andreas, who excelled at second-guessing those who surrounded him. She buried her head in his shoulder. He smoothed her hair. Handsome mouth taut, he closed his arms round her. If he were patient she would tell him what was wrong. She was quite incapable of keeping anything important from him. Her confiding habits were engrained, he reminded himself.

'I'm sorry…I suppose I've just come over all emotional thinking about our anniversary,' Hope mumbled in a muffled voice.

Lush black lashes lifted on guarded dark golden eyes. 'Anniversary?'

'Don't you know that in another few days we'll have been together for two whole years?' Hope lifted her tousled head, a happy smile of achievement on lips still swollen from his kisses. 'I want to celebrate it.'

Two years? His gaze narrowed, his lean, darkly handsome face impassive, concealing his stunned reaction to that news. Had she really been in his life that long? He was appalled that he had neglected to

notice her staggering longevity. Two years? Marriages
didn't last that long. When had she become the equivalent of a fixture? She had inserted herself into his
daily routine with astounding subtlety. She was just...
there. She didn't cling but the tendrils of her existence
were as meshed with his as ivy round a tree. That was
not an inspiring analogy. But when had he last slept
with another woman? He squashed the instant sliver
of guilt that even the thought ignited. He had been
incredibly faithful to her. Acknowledging that reality
set his even white teeth on edge. Inexplicable as it
seemed to him, she had infiltrated his freedom like an
invisible invading army and conditioned him in ways
that were foreign to him. Angry surprise turned him
to ice as though he were in the presence of the enemy.

'I'm not into anniversaries with women,' Andreas
delivered, brilliant eyes dark as coals and diamond-
bright. 'I don't do the sentimental stuff.'

Hope could hardly breathe. She wanted to put her
hand over his beautiful mouth and prevent him from
saying anything more. She could not bear that he
should fulfil any part of Vanessa's disparaging forecast, yet she was equally unable to let that laden silence lie. 'But it's special to me that you've been a
part of my life for so long.'

Andreas shrugged a muscular bronzed shoulder and
firmly lifted her off him. 'We have a good time together. I value you. But it would be inappropriate to
celebrate an anniversary. That's not what we're
about.'

Hope felt like someone tied to the railway tracks
in front of an express train and the roar of the metal
monster was his words crushing the dreams she had

cherished and ripping apart her illusions. In one lithe, powerful movement, he sprang off the bed and headed into the bathroom. She lay there cold and shocked and shattered. In her presence he had changed from the guy she loved into an intimidating stranger with cold eyes and a harsh, unfeeling voice and he had pushed her away. She got up to pull on the ice-blue wrap lying on a nearby chair. But she was forced to sink back down onto the bed because her head was swimming. It was that stupid dizziness again, she thought wearily. Perhaps it was an ear infection that was interfering with her sense of balance.

I value you. What sort of a declaration was that? That Andreas knew the exact extent of her worth? In terms of convenience? No, he didn't do sentimental but, perhaps more tellingly, he had not cared whether or not he wounded her feelings. He had to be very sure of her to put a blanket ban on even a minor celebration. Biting her lip and with a knot of fear forming inside her, Hope tightened the sash on her wrap. But anger was also slowly stirring out of the ashes of the hurt caused by his humiliating response to her perfectly innocent remarks.

Taut with angry, frustrated tension, Andreas leant back against the limestone wall in the power shower and let the water stream down over his magnificent bronzed body. Usually he was still in bed with Hope at this stage of the evening. His chill-out time with her had been wrecked. Taken by surprise, he had been tactless. He wanted to punch something. Their relationship was as near perfect as he had ever hoped to achieve on a casual basis. Hope never made unreasonable demands and appeared to have no greater ambition in life than to make him happy. And she was bloody brilliant at making him happy, Andreas acknowledged grudgingly. He did not want to lose her. But what did he do with a mistress who did not know she was a mistress? A mistress who wanted to celebrate anniversaries as if she were a wife? *Theos mou...* He winced. What had come over her?

Most probably, Andreas reasoned with a surge of fierce resentment, Hope's shrewish friend, Vanessa, was responsible. Was it she who had destroyed Hope's sunny contentment? Who else could it have been? Once or twice Hope had repeated Vanessa's revealingly acidic remarks about men. Andreas had gained the distinct impression that Hope's best friend would fry him alive in hot oil if she ever got the chance.

That his association with Hope should be so misjudged and so undervalued outraged Andreas. He was proud of the way he treated Hope. He looked after her. She was a very happy woman. Why? He kept all the nasty realities of life at bay. He even made her dreams come true. Although she had no suspicion of the fact, eighteen months earlier it had been his influence that had won her a place on a design course at a leading art college. Thanks to him she had since graduated and begun fashioning handbags that he was secretly convinced no sane woman would ever wish to buy. He had a shuddering recollection of the one shaped like a ripe tomato. But the point was, Hope was cheerfully content...or, at least, she had been until the serpent had entered Eden.

Andreas was towelling himself dry when Hope entered the bathroom. She drew in a slow, deep breath to steady herself and fixed turquoise blue eyes bravely on him. 'So if we can't have anniversaries, what can we have?'

Six feet four inches tall, black hair still wet from the shower and crystalline drops of water still sparkling on the ebony curls defining his powerful pectoral muscles, Andreas froze. He had not expected a second assault in that line. The first had been startling enough. Winged ebony brows drew together. 'I don't believe I follow...'

Hope realised that there was a lump in her throat, a lump that was swelling with every second that passed with the threat of tears. 'I...I suppose I'm asking is this it for you and me?'

'Clarify that,' Andreas instructed in the cool tone he used in the office to make underlings jump. But his dark golden eyes shimmered with intensity. He could not credit the idea but for a split second he wondered if she was threatening to dump him.

'Once you told me that nothing stays the same and that everything must progress,' Hope reminded him unsteadily. 'You said that the things that remain static wither and die. Yet from what I can see, in the last two years we haven't changed at all.'

Right there and then, Andreas decided that in the future it would be wiser to keep all words of wisdom on the score of goal-orientated achievement targets and healthy change to himself.

Every word Hope spoke came from her heart and nothing was pre-planned or judged for its effect. She was very upset. Horribly conscious of his cool distance, she was desperate to make sense of what was happening between them. She needed the reassurance of finding out exactly where she stood with the man she loved.

'So what about us?' Hope continued half under her breath, doggedly pushing the question out, refusing to surrender to her inner fears. 'Are we going anywhere?'

Incredulous that Hope should be subjecting him to such an onslaught, Andreas snatched in a charged breath and reached for her with determined hands. Gathering her small, curvaceous body to him, he reclaimed her mouth in a fierce, sweet invasion that left her quivering with disconcertion. 'Back to bed?' he murmured with hungry intent as he finally lifted his arrogant dark head.

Her pale face flamed as though he had slapped her. Indeed she felt as though he might as well have done, for she was bitterly ashamed that he had found it so easy to distract her. 'Is that my answer? I want to feel like I'm part of your life, not just someone you sleep with,' she confided painfully.

Golden eyes ablaze with displeasure, Andreas spread lean brown hands wide in emphasis. 'You *are* part of my life!'

'If that's true, why do I never get to meet your friends?' Her voice was rising with stress in spite of her efforts to keep it level. 'Are you ashamed of me?' she gasped strickenly.

'When we're together, I prefer to keep you to myself, *pedhi mou*. I won't apologise for that,' Andreas fielded smoothly. 'Calm yourself. You're getting hysterical!'

'I'm not...I'm just fighting with you!'

Andreas dealt her a stony appraisal. 'I won't fight with you.'

'Is that something else you're not into?' Hope heard herself hurl in shock at her own daring. Backing away from him, she jarred her hip painfully on a corner of the vanity unit behind her.

'Are you hurt?' Lean, strong face taut, Andreas strode forward.

In the room next door the phone started ringing. The untimely interruption made Andreas swear in exasperated Greek, but Hope was grateful for the excuse to escape and answer the call.

'Get me Andreas...' Elyssa Southwick's imperious voice demanded.

'Hold on, please,' Hope said gruffly.

If Elyssa couldn't raise Andreas on his mobile phone when he was in London, she called the apartment instead. The Nicolaidis siblings were close, for their parents had died when Elyssa was barely a teenager. Still only in her mid twenties, Elyssa leant heavily on her big brother for support. The young Greek woman, however, seemed to have no inkling of Hope's identity, for she always spoke to Hope as though she were a servant on telephone duty.

Andreas accepted the phone Hope extended. But his attention was on Hope, who looked like glass about to shatter, her warm blue eyes cast down and her generous mouth taut with strain. He was furious with her. Why was she doing this to them? The phone dialogue continued in Greek. Hope understood the gist of it for she had been learning the language at night class for many months and had planned to surprise Andreas with her proficiency. Elyssa was reminding her brother that she was throwing a housewarming party the next week. Hope left the room.

Of course, she would not be invited to the party. Andreas was in no hurry to take her out and show her off. Was that because he was only using her for sex?

Easy, uncomplicated sex with a woman who had been weak and foolish enough to give herself freely on that basis from the very outset of their acquaintance? How could she complain on that score when Andreas had never promised anything else and she had never had the courage to ask for anything more?

Pure anguish threatened to take hold of Hope. She wanted to weep and wail like a soul in torment and the power of her own distraught emotions scared her. Her mouth wobbled and she pinned it flat. Terrified as she was of breaking down while Andreas was still in the apartment, she fought to keep a lid on all distressing thoughts.

But her mind marched on with relentless cruelty. Andreas thought nothing of making love over and over again. He was all Greek, an unashamedly passionate guy with an insatiably high libido. But he was more into work than leisure and a woman who required little in terms of romance or attention was a necessity. No doubt, she suited him on those scores. She had always tried to be independent. She didn't create a fuss when he was late or business kept him from her. She had accepted her backstage role in his life.

Why? Andreas was so much what she was not and never could be. It was not that she suffered from low self-esteem; simply that she could not ignore or forget the reality that Andreas outranked her in so many ways. He was the gorgeous, sophisticated product of a world of immense privilege and even more immense wealth. If it rained on a summer day, he thought he was suffering and he had once flown her halfway across the world to spend three hours on a hot beach. He was highly educated and shockingly clever. Far too clever for his own good, she had often thought, she recalled ruefully, for he was a perfectionist, obsessively driven to achieve, but rarely satisfied even by superlative results.

What had she to offer in comparison? Basic schooling, an ordinary background and at best what she deemed to be only average looks and intelligence. How could she ever have dared to dream that some day he might fall in love with her? Or that he might eventually choose to offer her a more secure place in his life? But she had been guilty of harbouring exactly those dreams. She loved Andreas, she loved him a great deal, and right from the beginning that had been a handicap to any form of restraint or common sense.

Hope tilted up her chin as if she was bracing herself. Andreas might be satisfied with the current status quo, but she needed to have a good hard think about whether or not she could cope with a relationship that had no future. And presumably none of the commitment she had taken for granted that she already had. Her tummy flipped. She felt sick at the very idea that she might have to walk away from Andreas. But if she meant nothing more to him than a casual bed partner, wasn't that her only option?

On the other hand, was it possible that she had chosen the worst possible moment to mention something that Andreas seemed to find so controversial? Maybe the very word 'anniversary' struck horror into his bones. Maybe she was overreacting to her own anxieties, concerns that she had contrived to ignore until a friend had voiced similar reservations.

Here she was fighting with Andreas for the very first time. Here she was putting their entire relationship in jeopardy. Her hands knotted into fists and her eyes swam with hot tears. She never cried. What was the matter with her? So much emotion was swilling about inside her, she felt frighteningly on edge. She had almost shouted at him. He had been astonished. She pressed trembling hands to her cool cheeks. She breathed in slow and deep in an effort to recapture the tranquillity that had until very recent times been so much a part of her nature.

'Hope...' His long, lean, muscular body garbed only in a pair of cotton boxers, Andreas found her by the window in the elegant sitting room. Looking incredibly male and sexy, he strolled across the handsome oak-planked floor and closed firm hands over her knotted fingers to pull her close. His brilliant golden eyes snared her deeply troubled gaze and held her entrapped. 'How would you like to go to my sister's party next week?'

Her surprise and pleasure linked and swelled into a sensation of overwhelming joy and relief. 'Are you serious? My goodness, I'd love to go!'

Andreas watched the glow of happiness reanimate in the instant generous smile that lit up her face. Situation defused: it had been the right gesture to make. A weekend in Paris would have compromised his principles in regard to anniversaries. That Elyssa would barely notice Hope's existence among so many other guests was irrelevant. There was no reason why Hope should not attend, but he had no intention of making a habit of such invitations.

Eventually, he would have to do his duty by the Nicolaidis name and marry to father an heir. In the light of that prospect, it was wise to make a distinction between his public and his private life and be discreet. Hope would be hurt but, the longer she had been part of his life, the harder she would find it to break away and the more easily she would adjust to the inevitable restrictions and accept them, Andreas reflected with hard determination.

Her heart beating very fast, Hope curved into the gloriously familiar heat of his big, powerful frame. She felt very guilty over her temporary loss of faith in him. Obviously, she should have spoken up sooner. Perhaps he had just needed a little nudge in the right direction.

'Now…' Long brown fingers curved to her cheekbones and her breath began coming in quick shallow bursts. His scorching golden eyes dazzled her. Excitement leapt even before he tasted her readily parted lips with devastating hunger and swept her up into his arms to carry her back to the bedroom.

CHAPTER TWO

ENTERING the imposing mansion that Elyssa and her wealthy husband, Finlay Southwick, had renovated at reputedly vast expense, Hope smoothed her V-necked black dress down over her hips with damp palms.

The party was already in full swing, for Andreas did not believe in early arrivals. She was very nervous and was resisting a powerful urge to stick to him like superglue. She had been so scared of wearing the wrong thing that she had opted to play it safe with black, but women all around her were wearing rainbow colours and she felt horribly drab and unadventurous. In addition, her plan to spend half the day grooming herself to her personal best in the presentation stakes had been interrupted, cast into confusion and pretty much destroyed by Andreas arriving three hours early.

Warm colour blossomed in Hope's cheeks. A business meeting had been cancelled, leaving Andreas free to finish early. The intimate ache between her thighs testified to the enthusiasm with which Andreas had taken advantage of that rare gift of extra time with her.

A youthful blonde caught up in the crush stared at Hope in surprise and stopped dead. 'It *is* you, isn't it? You're the handbag lady who does the stall in Camden market…aren't you?'

'I think you will find that you are mistaken,'

Andreas interposed in a cool, deflating tone that would have crushed granite.

Hope tensed. The teenager already reddening with embarrassment had vaguely familiar features. 'Yes... that's me,' she confirmed with a warm smile to ease the girl's discomfiture.

'My mother adores the bag I gave her for her birthday and loads of her friends are desperate to find out where she got it from! I'll be calling back soon,' the blonde promised.

Before Hope could confide that she had given up on selling at the market, Andreas had curved a firm hand to her spine to urge her past. The foyer was big and crowded with noisy knots of chattering guests. He pressed her into a doorway to say in an icy undertone, 'Is it true? Have you been flogging merchandise from a stall?'

Taken aback, Hope looked up at him in dismay. His gleaming dark eyes were hard and cold. 'Yes. Initially, I was doing market research to find out what sells to which age groups. It helped me keep in touch with current trends—'

'You've been keeping a market stall,' Andreas sliced in, cold, incredulous disapproval etched into the hard angles of his lean, strong face. 'Trading in the street as though you were penniless and without means of support! How *dare* you affront me in such a manner?'

Hope was paralysed to the spot. Astonishment had leached all the natural colour from below her skin. 'It never occurred to me that you might be so snobbish about it,' she muttered unevenly.

'I am not a snob.' Andreas rejected that accusation out of hand.

Anxious turquoise eyes clear as glass rested on him. 'I'm afraid you are, but with your privileged background that's perfectly normal and understandable—'

'*Theos*…what has my background to do with this?' Andreas grated, his annoyance fuelled to anger by the expression of gentle and compassionate forgiveness that she wore. 'Why did you not tell me that you were working as a street trader?'

'For goodness' sake, it was only an occasional casual thing. I had no idea you would feel like this about it. I didn't even think that you would be interested,' Hope murmured unhappily. 'As it happens, I'm not doing the market any more—'

'You should never have stooped to such a level. From now on you will respect the standards required to conserve your dignity.' Devastatingly handsome features set in grim lines of intimidating impassivity, Andreas reined back his temper with difficulty.

'I don't think I've got any to conserve,' Hope confided apologetically, deciding that it might not be the best time to tell him that she had only given up the market in favour of craft fairs.

Sometimes, the cocoon of his own stratospheric wealth made Andreas hopelessly impractical, she thought ruefully. After all, she *was* virtually penniless. She had lived like a church mouse on her student loan and had since stretched her meagre earnings to paying for all her outgoings but it was a real uphill battle. Only the fact that she had no rent to pay for the roof over her head had enabled her to manage. Was he even aware of the contribution she made to the household bills? Or did one of his staff deal with all his domestic expenditure at the apartment?

'But I *have*, so cultivate dignity for my benefit,' Andreas delivered with cutting clarity, refusing to be softened by the playful light in her gaze.

His pride was outraged by the very idea of her rubbing shoulders with market traders and serving customers. Such a milieu was beneath her touch and she ought to know that without being told. She was too naive and she lacked discrimination. How much over-familiarity and coarseness had she endured without complaint? What other foolish things did she get up to that he didn't know about? His unquestioning trust in her was shaken. For the first time he acknowledged the inherent flaw in his own all too regular absences abroad. If he had been around more, he would have found out about the market-trading project and he would have suppressed it. In the future he would need to take a much closer interest in her activities.

Hope knew Andreas too well not to recognise his distaste and it cut her to the quick at a moment when she was already feeling vulnerable. He was disappointed in her. It was plain that he believed she had embarrassed him and that really hurt. The cool distance stamped in his stunning dark golden eyes hit her hardest of all.

At that point she registered that the crush had magically cleared to allow them a clear passage. But she was discomfited by the discovery that they appeared to be the cynosure of all eyes. A perceptible ripple of excited awareness was travelling round the big reception room, turning every head in their direction. Eyes skimmed over her with curiosity but lingered with fascinated awe on the tall, authoritative male at her side. Andreas was the main attraction and the crowds parted before him as though he were royalty. Certainly, he was royally indifferent to the power of his own presence. He ignored all but a tiny number of the hopeful and gushing greetings angled at him.

A beautiful young woman with sultry dark eyes and long brown hair, her slender figure displayed to advantage in a strappy iridescent pink dress, was hurrying towards them. Hope, who had often seen photos of Elyssa in gossip magazines, recognised Andreas's sister instantly and smiled. Her tummy felt tight with nerves. She so much wanted her meeting with the other woman to go well. Elyssa focused her attention on her brother and kissed him on both cheeks in ebullient welcome even as she uttered a spirited barrage of complaint about his late arrival.

Untouched by that censure, indeed laughing, Andreas flicked a glance at Hope as though he was about to introduce her to his sibling. However, a heavily built older man approached him just then and addressed him in a flood of Greek. 'Excuse me a moment,' Andreas said to both women, his mouth tightening with impatience as he stepped to one side.

'I'm Hope,' Hope confided as she extended a friendly hand to Elyssa. 'I've been looking forward to meeting you.'

A glittering smile pinned to her burgundy-tinted mouth, Elyssa fixed sullen dark eyes on her, ignored her hand and murmured with stinging scorn, 'You're my brother's whore. Why would *I* want to meet *you*?'

As Elyssa walked away, her smile brighter than ever, Hope struggled to conceal her shock. Her face burning, she was gripped by a sick sense of humiliation. That Andreas's sister and closest relative, a woman who did not even know her, should attack her with such venom appalled her. She told herself that she would not think about the offensive label the brunette had applied to her. She had been mad keen to come to Elyssa's party, she reminded herself doggedly, and she had to make the best of the event for Andreas's sake. Andreas was very fond of his kid sister. There was no way she could tell him what Elyssa had said to her. She would just have to take it on the chin.

Across the room, a man in his twenties with fair, angelic features at odds with his bloodshot eyes and tousled spiky blond hair raised his hand to her in nonchalant greeting. Grateful to see a face she knew in that sea of daunting strangers, Hope beamed at him.

'Do you know who that guy is?' Andreas enquired flatly.

'Ben Campbell…he's Vanessa's cousin,' Hope told him, her face shadowing as she once again fought off the recollection of the name Elyssa had applied to her. *Whore*…no, she refused to even think about that.

Andreas spared the younger man a chilling glance and made no effort to acknowledge him. Campbell had a sleazy reputation for wild parties and indiscriminate womanising. He was very much disconcerted by the evident fact that Hope should be on friendly terms with him.

'I don't want you associating with Campbell,' Andreas imparted with succinct clarity.

Hope stiffened in surprise, chewed at her lower lip and then dropped her pale head. When had Andreas begun to talk as though his every word, unreasonable or otherwise, ought to be her command? She might only have met Ben a few times but she liked him.

'Which means,' Andreas extended very dryly, for

he was less than impressed by her lack of response and the way she appeared to be avoiding his gaze, 'as of now, you no longer know him.'

Hope said nothing. How could she cut Ben dead and offend her best friend? Apart from anything else, it would be ridiculous overkill for a casual acquaintance that only encompassed a handful of meetings at Vanessa's apartment.

A woman glittering with diamonds swam up to speak to Andreas. She paid Hope the barest minimum of attention and was the forerunner in a long and constant procession of people frantic to get a chance to talk to him. In comparison, Hope felt as interesting as a wooden chair and would not have been surprised to find coats being draped over her.

Her confidence already smashed to bits by her hostess, Hope retreated into an alcove nearby. From that safe harbour, she watched the female contingent gush and flatter and hang on every word that fell from Andreas's beautifully sculpted lips. The men were loud with nerves, unerringly deferential and eager to hear his opinion.

His whore. Without the slightest warning, that dreadful tag leapt back into her mind and had much the same effect on her as an axe wielded by a maniac. A whore was a promiscuous woman, she thought sickly. A woman who bartered sex for reward. A woman who made a special effort to please men sexually. Could she be described in those terms?

Andreas did not give her money, but she lived in an apartment worthy of a princess and it did rejoice in a designer décor, fancy furniture and fantastic art works. Even if she worked a thousand years she would never be able to afford such luxury on her own income. But she was not promiscuous. When she had met Andreas, she had been a virgin. She had only ever slept with Andreas. He had taught her everything she knew. But Andreas being Andreas and a demanding perfectionist in all fields had doubtless ensured that she had learnt exactly what pleased him in bed. Did that make her a whore?

Feeling claustrophobic in her dim corner and too tormented by her own fears to stay still, Hope wandered off into the next room. Only then did she appreciate that her eyes were awash with tears. Ashamed of her lack of self-control, she hurried on in her exploration of the big, crowded house, afraid that if she lingered anywhere someone would notice that her emotions had got on top of her. A sob was clogging up her throat. She wished she had never come to the party. She felt duly punished for daring to crave what she had naively believed would be an important stepping stone in her relationship with Andreas. Finding herself alone in a quiet branch corridor, she paused, listened outside a solid panelled door and, reassured by the silence within, pressed down the handle.

The door creaked wide on a low-lit room and a startling spectacle. Andreas's sister, Elyssa, was passionately kissing a dark-haired man, who bore no resemblance whatsoever to her husband, Finlay Southwick.

Consternation momentarily froze Hope on the threshold. Shocked eyes veiling, she pulled the door closed again in a nerveless harried movement and sucked in air to steady herself. But before she could even breathe out again and move on, the door flew open again to reveal Elyssa.

'Don't you *dare* tell Andreas!' the young Greek woman hissed in a tempestuous mix of revealing fear and fury. 'If this gets back to my brother, I'll know who to blame and I'll destroy you!'

Barely able to credit the extent of the other woman's aggression, Hope murmured tightly, 'There's no need to threaten me—'

'There's every need,' Elyssa condemned furiously. 'What were you doing snooping? Did you follow me in here?'

'Of course I didn't!' Hope protested in disbelief. 'I wasn't snooping either. I was just looking for somewhere quiet where I could sit down. I thought the room was empty—'

'Did you really?' Elyssa sneered.

'Yes, I did. Look, I have no intention of telling anybody anything. I always mind my own business—'

'Just you see that you do, you fat cow!' the enraged brunette spat at her spitefully.

Reeling from that second attack, Hope walked away with a rigid back. Tears were blinding her: it was a nightmare party with the hostess from hell. She cannoned into someone and looked up with a stifled apology to focus on Ben Campbell.

'What's up?' Ben asked, his voice a trifle slurred.

'Nothing!' Brushing past him, Hope took refuge in the cloakroom. Secure then from prying ears and eyes, she punched out Vanessa's number on her mobile phone and said wretchedly, 'Everything's going horribly wrong. Elyssa hated me on sight!'

'Good. Andreas must be even keener than I suspected,' her friend responded with disconcerting good cheer.

'How do you make that out?' Hope swallowed back another sob and decided that she did indeed look very large in the black dress. All that dark unbroken colour was less than flattering. In fact her reflection seemed to fill the whole dainty mirror above the vanity unit.

'Elyssa's a spoilt little brat of an heiress and she's possessive of her big brother. She must have some idea how long you've been with him and I bet she's worried that he's serious. Did she say anything nasty? Anything you could make decent mileage out of?'

Hope frowned, for where Andreas's sister was concerned she felt honour-bound to preserve a discreet silence. 'Why?'

'Because you could use it as ammunition and confide tearfully in Andreas. Only a week ago, I would have said that that was a major no-no, but with impressively little effort you miraculously persuaded Andreas to take you to the party of the year,' the redhead mused thoughtfully. 'I'm now convinced that you have more influence over Andreas Nicolaidis than either he or you appreciate.'

'Do you really think so?' Hope encouraged, desperate to have her spirits raised even with what she deemed to be a false hope. 'But I wouldn't dream of saying anything that would cause trouble between Andreas and his sister. That would be dreadfully mean of me and certain to fail—'

'If Elyssa is planning to be your enemy, you may not have much choice,' Vanessa warned.

'Don't be so pessimistic.' Hope sighed. 'She may well think that I'm not good enough for her brother—'

'Oh, please, don't start making excuses for her!' Vanessa groaned in despair.

Finishing the call, Hope returned the phone to her bag. She hadn't been able to bring herself to tell her best friend that she had been called a whore. She was too afraid that Vanessa might secretly think that Elyssa had had some justification for voicing that cruelly humiliating opinion. Emerging from the cloakroom, she saw that Ben was now lounging up against the wall a few feet away.

'Let's talk...' he urged, holding out a languid and rather wavering hand, which made her suspect that he was drunk. 'Who stole your big happy smile? I want you to tell me what's wrong. Van would kill me for walking by on the other side.'

Cheeks hot with self-consciousness as envious female eyes locked to her, Hope hurried over. 'Shush... there's nothing wrong...please keep your voice down—'

Ben locked both arms round her as much to keep himself upright, she suspected, as to prevent her walking away. 'Would you like me to take you home?'

'Thank you but no—'

'I got droves of women,' Ben confided lazily, bloodshot green eyes mocking her as she blushed and attempted to tug free of his hold. 'Do you think I could seduce you away from your Greek billionaire?'

'No chance. Nothing and nobody could,' Hope swore with fervour.

'Never say never...it's like challenging fate.' Scanning her pale, troubled expression, Ben sighed and dropped an almost paternal kiss down on top of her head. 'You're way too sweet and straight for Nicolaidis.'

Andreas was the restive centre of a crowd. He was bored: even at a distance she could tell. His stunning dark golden eyes picked her out when she was still moving towards him. Lean, extravagantly handsome face intent, he abandoned his audience without hesitation and strode forward to intercept her. 'Where the hell have you been?' he demanded.

'When the dialogue turns to gold prices and pork bellies, I feel a bit surplus to requirements.'

'Let's go, *pedhi mou*.' Closing a determined hand over hers, Andreas trailed her in the direction of the hall and remained wonderfully impervious to every fawning attempt to slow down his progress. 'We should never have got out of bed...'

As he hurried her down the steps into the cool night air the shameless sexual sizzle in his skimming appraisal made her tummy clench and her mouth run dry. Suddenly everything that had upset her seemed utterly unimportant. She loved him to death. What else mattered? In a spontaneous movement, she stretched up on her tiptoes to press a kiss to a bronzed cheekbone and she breathed in the heady male scent of his skin with the delight of an addict.

'Andreas? Please wait,' a soft voice interposed from behind them in Greek. 'I need to speak to you.'

Andreas tensed, ebony brows drawing together. He tucked Hope into the waiting limousine with scrupulous care and an apologetic smile. 'Give me five minutes...I'll say your goodbyes for you.'

Elyssa's approach had made Hope tense as well, but she was grateful to be released from the challenge of dealing with his volatile sister again. She had been surprised at how quiet and hesitant the brunette had sounded until it occurred to her that perhaps Elyssa

intended to confide in her brother and admit that all
was not well in her marriage. Hope liked that idea,
for she felt bad about withholding what she had seen
from Andreas. After all, he was very attached to his
sister and her two young children. Cynical he might
be, but Hope was convinced that he would make considerable effort to keep his sister's family together.

Perhaps Elyssa, who had married when she was
still very young, had allowed a flirtation to get out of
hand. Whatever, Hope reminded herself that the situation was none of her business. But even so the
whole wretched tangle was liable to put Andreas in a
very bad mood. Andreas was not tolerant of female
mistakes in the fidelity line, Hope reflected ruefully.
More than once she had heard him pass distinctly
judgemental comments on that score.

It was fifteen minutes before Andreas joined her.
In the artificial light his vibrant olive skin tone had
an unusually pale aspect. His brilliant eyes were dark
and screened to a brooding glitter. Convinced that his
sister had told him what had happened, Hope was
unsurprised by his silence during the drive back
through the city streets. He was fiercely loyal to his
own flesh and blood and he had never discussed
Elyssa with her.

When Hope recognised the tension in the atmosphere, she thought she had to be imagining it. Then
doubt crept in. Had Elyssa accused her of snooping?
Surely Andreas was too sensible to pay credence to
that far-fetched idea? Her brow tightened even more
with tension.

In the lift on the way up to the apartment, she met
bold dark eyes cold as the Atlantic in winter. 'What's
the matter?' she asked instantly.

'Why are you asking?' Andreas murmured sibilantly.

Hope had never heard that daunting inflection in his rich dark drawl before. Entering the hall, she kicked off her shoes as was her wont and hesitated.

'Hope…?'

Slowly she turned round and stared back at him. Andreas was still lodged at the far side of the spacious hall. Lethally tall and exotically dark and sexy, he looked so drop-dead gorgeous he took her breath away. Yet her sense of being under threat at that moment was so intense that she felt slightly queasy.

Andreas strolled fluidly towards her. Brilliant dark eyes flashed shimmering gold. 'Did anything happen tonight that you would like to tell me about?'

CHAPTER THREE

HOPE gulped. Why was Andreas acting as if she had done something wrong? She had no desire to whinge about Elyssa's unkindness or indeed to tell tales about the younger woman. Yet if Andreas knew that she had seen his sister with another man, why was he making a mystery of that embarrassing event?

'No, nothing comes to mind,' Hope answered uneasily, wishing she did not feel quite so guilty about keeping quiet on Elyssa's behalf.

'You were seen with Ben Campbell,' Andreas imparted icily, but there was a dauntingly rough and unfamiliar edge to his intonation.

Disconcerted by that reference to Ben, Hope turned pink and shifted uncomfortably, but she could see no reason to be the slightest bit apologetic on that score. 'Yes, I did speak to Ben for a couple of minutes.'

'Finlay, my brother-in-law, saw you with him. You were in Campbell's arms.'

That particular choice of wording sent a stab of sincere annoyance travelling through Hope. Could something so minor and innocent in every way be responsible for causing so much bad feeling? She had not even met Elyssa's husband. But she could not help thinking that there was surely something rather mean-spirited about a man capable of reading anything suspect into her brief chat with Ben. 'It wasn't quite as you make it sound—'

Andreas elevated a black brow. 'Wasn't it?'

Her usual calm chipping away at an ever-faster rate, Hope stared back at him in an effort to comprehend the mystery of his unusual behaviour. He had never shown signs of being unreasonably jealous or possessive. Now all of a sudden he was acting like a stranger. 'Of course it wasn't. For a start there were at least half a dozen other people nearby,' she pointed out. 'Ben wasn't even flirting with me, he was just fooling around.'

His lean bronzed features remained maddeningly uninformative. 'Was he?'

'For goodness' sake, Andreas,' Hope continued with gathering force, for a cascade of little mental alarm bells was beginning to go off inside her head. 'Ben probably put his arms round me because he had to hang onto me to stay upright. He *was* rather merry. There certainly wasn't anything else to it. In fact, I'm finding it very hard to believe that we're having this conversation.'

'We're having this conversation because five minutes after Finlay saw you getting cosy in public with Campbell, Elyssa surprised you getting cosier still in private,' Andreas delivered with grim clarity.

Hope stilled, the animated pink draining slowly from her shaken face. 'Say that again...'

'Surely I don't need to repeat it,' Andreas said, his disgust unconcealed. 'You went into a private room with Campbell.'

A tiny pulse had begun to go bang-bang-bang at Hope's temple and she was so stiff she might have been fashioned out of stone. 'I did not go into any room to be alone with Ben—'

Something flashed in his hard, dark gaze: a sizzle of golden fury. 'This is grubby...this is beneath me!'

Andreas incised with a raw, slashing derision that cut her to the bone. 'At least admit the truth. When such behaviour is witnessed, there is no scope to lie or make excuses.'

'But I'm not lying or making excuses,' Hope fielded breathlessly, for sheer shock was making her feel as if she had been punched squarely in the solar plexus. 'What am I supposed to have been doing with Ben?'

'You were kissing him—'

'I wasn't!' Hope gasped. 'Your sister is—'

Andreas spread his arms in a sudden violent movement that shook her into silence. 'Don't offend me even more by daring to question my sister's integrity. She saw what she saw. You abused her hospitality and embarrassed her.'

'I did not...I *swear* I did not,' Hope muttered in bewilderment, her head swimming with too many thoughts at once. As she finally grasped how cruelly manipulative and unashamedly deceitful Elyssa Southwick had been, she felt sick to the stomach. For an instant she was simply shattered that someone she barely knew could be prepared to tell a lie of such appalling magnitude about her.

'Elyssa was very upset and she didn't know what to do. But after discussing the matter with her husband, she decided that I had a right to know that you were behaving like a slut behind my back!' Andreas bit out rawly, his wintry cool and control starting to crack.

Hope trembled. 'But it's not true. Not a word of it is true—'

'I want to hear you admit the truth before I leave. You owe me that at the very least,' Andreas growled.

Even as she saw that her world was falling apart, Hope was sickly fascinated by the callous ruthlessness that Elyssa had employed to bring about the destruction she had threatened. 'I've been a real fool,' she mumbled in a daze. 'I always try to overlook other people's mistakes and not stand in judgement because I know I'm not perfect either. But I overlooked one very dangerous fact…your sister is as clever as you are and it seems she decided that I was a threat to her security.'

His handsome mouth curled. 'That's offensive nonsense. Have the decency to leave Elyssa out of this unpleasant business.'

'I don't think I can.' Yet Hope was also asking herself how she could possibly stage a creditable counter-accusation. Having got her story in first, Elyssa had backed it up most impressively with her husband's reference to having previously seen Hope in Ben Campbell's arms. It didn't matter that that latter incident had taken place in the most innocent of circumstances. The other man's additional testimony had made the case against Hope look irrefutable. On the other hand, she reasoned, perhaps the story might have looked unarguable to a stranger, but should Andreas not know her better?

'Don't you know me better than this?' she whispered out loud.

That question hit Andreas as hard as a blast of dynamite detonating inside a giant rock. Rage was like a clenched-tight fist inside him and it took all his concentration to keep it contained. He could not stand to look at her; yet somehow he could not make himself look away. He had trusted her. Until his sister had blown away his illusions he had had no idea just how deep his trust in Hope had run. The sleazy truth had come as a body blow. But then placing that amount of faith in a mistress was asking for trouble, he reflected bitterly. He had kept her around too long. He had let her rosy, cosy sentimentality infect him like a virus and blur the boundaries of what they shared: great sex, nothing more, and he could find equally great sex elsewhere.

'Andreas?' Hope breathed unevenly, a tumult of emotions thrust down as she fought a fierce battle not to lose control. 'Do you really think that I would do something like that?'

Insolent golden eyes zeroed in on her. 'Is it beyond impossible?' Andreas drawled smooth as silk. 'You did it with me in a barn the first night we met.'

All the natural colour bled from Hope's complexion to leave her pale as parchment. Pain exploded inside her. But on some level, she welcomed the hurt inflicted by his cruel derision. Perhaps it was a long overdue punishment for her recklessness that night. Evidently that bad beginning had come back to haunt her. He didn't respect her; he had obviously never respected her. Virgin or not, she had been too easy a conquest and he was now looking back at that as though it had been the first betraying symptom of her being a slut in the making. It was incredibly cruel of him to throw that first night back in her teeth. She had cherished the memory of the night she fell in love with him as the very essence of romance. But he had slung that same recollection back to her as a base and humiliating insult.

Her eyes felt horribly hot, dry and scratchy. Shock seemed to have driven all desire to cry out of her.

'Yes I did, didn't I?' she managed gruffly. 'But even if it wasn't special for you, it was for me.'

Emanating pure indifference on that issue, Andreas shrugged a broad shoulder in a gesture that was as careless as it was wounding.

Hope tried again. 'You have to listen to me—'

'No, I don't.'

'I didn't do anything tonight and I'm not lying to you. I have never kissed Ben Campbell,' Hope declared with vehemence.

'I expect you to find alternative accommodation by the end of the month. It's over,' Andreas countered with supreme derision.

Hope realised he was about to leave and horror galvanised her out of her paralysis into sudden action. She placed herself between Andreas and the front door. 'You can't leave!'

'Watch me—'

'No, I won't. I want you to stop and think about the person you know me to be. Ask yourself if I'd throw what we have away just for the chance to snog Ben Campbell!'

His strong jaw line clenched. 'Other women have. He's wrecked several marriages with his little-boy-lost act. He's also famous for going after women who belong to other men—'

'But I don't fancy him…I never have. I imagine half of London has got to snog Ben when he's drunk. He's not exactly exclusive,' Hope pointed out in growing desperation, praying that the very tenor of her comments would force Andreas to see that she had never even thought of Ben Campbell as a potentially fanciable male. All he had ever been on her terms was Vanessa's rather dissolute and amusing cousin. 'If you won't believe me, ask Ben if anything happened tonight.'

Outraged by that suggestion, Andreas vented a harsh laugh of incredulity. 'Why would I lower myself to that level? Had you been my wife, I would have confronted him. I would've torn him apart for daring to lay a single finger on you!' he proclaimed with a disconcertingly vicious edge to his dark, deep drawl. 'But you're *not* my wife, you're my mistress and, as such, expendable with the minimum of fuss.'

Ashen-pale beneath the lash of his naked contempt, Hope looked back at him, distraught turquoise eyes sparkling with sudden angry denial. 'I am not and I have never been your mistress.'

'Then what are you?' Andreas purred like a panther ready to flex his claws and draw blood.

'A woman who fell in love with you and who never stopped to count the cost,' Hope quantified jerkily, her generous mouth compressing. 'Some people would judge me harshly enough for that or call me a fool. But that doesn't make me your mistress—'

'A lot of women have told me they loved me,' Andreas murmured with sizzling scorn. 'Invariably they love what I can give them more.'

Her spine ached with tension. 'But I've never let you give me anything. With the exception of this apartment, I've kept your money out of our relationship and I never once looked for or accepted expensive gifts. Don't try to bundle me up with other women when I've always been true to you!' she told him, hearing the sharp, accusing undertone in her voice and unable to suppress it. 'And you can also stop insulting me for what I haven't done and talking at me in that bored, sneering way!'

'If I stop sneering, I might lose my temper,' Andreas asserted with a lethal quietness that made gooseflesh prickle at the nape of her neck. 'Now get out of my way...I'm leaving.'

Hope backed up against the door in a panic. 'Over my dead body. I won't let you leave until you listen to me. This is like a living nightmare and I won't let it happen to us—'

'There is no us now.' Without further ado, Andreas lifted her bodily out of his path and strode through the door.

Hope could not believe he was gone any more easily than she could accept what had just happened. Only a few hours earlier when they had left for the party, she had been so happy and secure. To accept that Andreas had dumped her, walked out on her, indeed finished with her absolutely and for ever was more than she could bear to deal with at that moment.

Like someone lost in a strange land, she wandered round the big, empty apartment. Elyssa had told horrible lies about her. Such behaviour was so inexplicable to Hope that for the space of an hour she strove frantically to plan out how she might approach Andreas's sister and what she might say to persuade the young Greek woman that she had to retract her false accusation. But even an optimist like Hope could not cling to such a remote prospect for long.

After all, even before she had had the misfortune to catch Elyssa in compromising circumstances, Elyssa had made it clear that she despised her. The brunette had too much to lose from telling the truth and had triumphed with her lies. She had managed to destroy Hope's relationship with her brother and ensure that Hope was banished from his life.

Hope's hands closed tight in on themselves. She recognised that she was still in a stupor of shock. But she was already thinking that she ought to have told Andreas that she had seen his sister with another man. Whether he believed her side of the story or not, she needed to speak up in her own defence. Yet what realistic chance of success did she have? Any attempt she made to clear her own name would entail accusing Elyssa of, not only being a liar, but also being an unfaithful wife. She shivered at the prospect. Andreas was very proud and protective of his younger sister. Honour and family were all-important to the Greek male. Any attack on Elyssa would outrage him.

She tripped over the black shirt lying discarded by the bed and swept it up, burying her face in its crumpled cotton folds to draw in the scent of Andreas. He was gone. How could someone who felt like the other half of her leave and how could she still function? Terror spread into the void inside her for she could not imagine living without Andreas. A passion of grief dug nasty talon claws into her shrinking flesh. Her aching eyes finally overflowed and she threw herself down on the bed and cried until her throat hurt and she could hardly see through her swollen eyes. In the silence that followed, she was overwhelmed by a terrible sense of loss and emptiness.

In the limo that ferried him back to the town house, Andreas worked his way through two brandies. What Elyssa had seen admitted no possibility of error. Hope's foolish pleas of innocence had only deepened his anger. He concentrated on that anger, letting it rise like a red mist and suppress all other thoughts. He would prove that she was lying, he decided grimly.

Lifting the phone, he called his security chief and, with a perfunctory apology for the late hour, he requested a detailed rundown of Hope's daily itinerary in recent months.

Somewhere around dawn, Hope had drifted into an uneasy slumber disturbed by dreams. Wakening, she sat up, and as the awful events of the previous night rolled back to her her tummy seemed to roll queasily in concert. In the aftermath of that rare bout of nausea, she stumbled into the shower and slumped. With or without Andreas, her life had to go on, she reminded herself dully. There was no point being wimpy about it. From somewhere she had to find the strength to concentrate on the practicalities of life. She had to find somewhere else to live. It was also time to redouble her so-far-unsuccessful efforts to get a loan that would enable her to set up her own business. When she was finally in a position to design and produce her own small select line of handbags, she would be working night and day. Yes, she would be so incredibly busy she wouldn't have the time to agonise over Andreas.

She noticed a small decorative gold box resting on a console table in the hall. When he'd arrived the day before, Andreas had tossed something down before he'd hauled her into his arms. As always it would be chocolate, superlative, incredible, melt-in-the-mouth chocolate purchased abroad at an extortionate price. And as well? Opening the box, she lifted out the tiny gold charm that he had included as a surprise. Only it wasn't really a surprise any more for one by one Andreas had given her an entire collection of unusual charms for her bracelet. This particular one was her name picked out with tiny glittering stones. Some lucky charm this one had proved to be...*hope*? Without warning her eyes flooded again and she squeezed them tight shut in an agony of loss. Blinking back tears, she realised that misery appeared to have deprived her of her usual love of chocolate. Instead the image of an olive and the prospect of that sharp rather than sweet taste came to mind and her taste buds watered. Bemused, for she had never liked olives, she frowned, but a moment later she headed into the kitchen.

On the way to the airport and a flight to New York, Andreas studied the security reports that detailed Hope's recent movements. His initial sensation of complete disbelief swiftly mounted to hot-blooded fury. He knew that if he put his private jet on hold he would never make his transatlantic meeting in time. But for once, emotion took strong precedence over efficiency and discipline and he told his chauffeur to turn round and head for the apartment instead.

Hope disposed of the now-empty jar of olives that Andreas had recently disdained to eat. Perhaps being sick had done something odd to her taste buds, she was reasoning in some confusion just as she heard the slam of the front door. Her heart leapt into her mouth and instant optimism seized her in a heady tide. Andreas had come back...Andreas had realised that she could never have been unfaithful to him!

'I'm down in the bedroom!' she called when she heard him say her name with all the impatience that was so much a part of his abrasive character.

Pale blonde hair tumbling round her shoulders in silken disarray, Hope focused turquoise eyes bright with expectation on the doorway and wished she had had time to get dressed and do something about the redness of her eyes. Her restive hands fiddled with the sash of her wrap.

Stunning golden eyes blazing, Andreas strode in. Garbed in a dark designer suit that accentuated his superb masculine physique, he looked heartbreakingly handsome. In a gesture of high voltage intensity that she would never have associated with his cool, controlled nature, he pitched a whole handful of documents down on the carpet at her feet. 'You lying slut!' he raked at her in raw condemnation. 'You've visited Campbell's apartment on countless occasions! You've even stayed the night there. You've been screwing him for months!'

Dumbfounded by the naked aggression of that full-frontal verbal attack, Hope was paralysed to the spot. 'What on earth are you talking about?' she framed in bewilderment. 'I've never been in Ben's apartment. I don't even know where he lives.'

'Like hell you don't! Take a good look at the quality of the evidence I have!' Andreas enunciated from between even white teeth.

'Evidence?' Hope bent down to lift several of the sheets of paper and frown down at the neat lines of computerised entries. 'What are these?'

'Surprise…surprise. You've had round-the-clock security for most of the past year. Those are the most recent reports of your activities,' Andreas informed her grittily.

'I've had round-the-clock security?' Hope parroted in total astonishment. 'Are you saying you've been having me watched?'

'I would argue that watched *over* would be a more fair and accurate description.'

'Who's been watching me?' Hope queried tightly, the physical recoil of genuine revulsion assailing her at the very thought of strangers taking note of her every move while she went about her daily business in sublime ignorance of their presence in her life.

'One of my own security teams. Top-notch professionals, who can do the job without attracting attention or interfering with your freedom. They don't make mistakes,' Andreas declared in a ferocious undertone, 'so don't waste your time trying that line on me.'

Hope surveyed him with huge perturbed eyes. 'I'm horrified that you could have distrusted me to that extent. You actually paid people to spy on me. That's absolutely horrible.'

The faintest tinge of dark colour demarcated the angular bronzed planes of the aristocratic cheekbones that enhanced his superb bone structure. 'That isn't how it was. Anonymous threats were made against me. Naturally I was concerned that through your association with me you could be at risk. I considered it my duty to protect you and I *did*. End of story.'

Hope wasn't listening. She was very much shocked by what he had revealed. 'The very idea that strangers have been spying on me gives me the creeps. I never realised until now just how much I took my right to privacy for granted.'

The confrontation was travelling along unanticipated lines that were utterly infuriating Andreas. How dared she focus on a trivial and obscure angle and ignore the giant sin of her own infidelity? What the hell was her right to privacy worth when set beside the gross betrayal of her affair with another man? Where did she get the nerve to look at him in that reproachful way as if he had done something shameful?

'Until last night I never once requested a copy of the reports on your movements. I *did* respect your privacy one hundred per cent,' Andreas countered with grim exactitude, his sculpted masculine mouth firming. 'But I wanted to satisfy myself with the proof of your infidelity. The number of visits you have made to Campbell's apartment corroborated the accusation made against you in full.'

Hope was still studying the papers in her hand. A slight sound was impelled from her parted lips when she recognised the familiar address that appeared several times over in the daily reports. She began to understand how the latest misunderstanding had come about. She breathed in deep, glancing up with rueful turquoise eyes to say quietly, 'Ben does own that apartment. But he throws a lot of parties and the residents' committee made life difficult for him. He moved out last year and Vanessa lives there now.'

Andreas was unmoved. Hard-as-granite golden eyes clashed with hers. 'I don't believe you. But I've no doubt that your best friend would back up a cover story for your benefit.'

On that score he could not have been more wrong. Having grown up with parents who had frequently cheated on each other, Vanessa heartily despised the deceit that went hand in hand with infidelity. She was the last woman alive likely to lie to conceal a friend's affair.

Taken aback as she was by Andreas's instant dismissal of her explanation about the apartment, Hope swallowed hard. She was very pale. '*Vanessa* lives at that address,' she stressed in her determination to make him listen. 'I hardly know Ben Campbell and I have not been unfaithful to you. I appreciate how dreadful all this must look to you but surely the two years we've been together at least buys me the right to a fair hearing—'

Andreas studied her with raw contempt. 'It buys you nothing.'

He swung on his heel and strode out of the bedroom.

'Wait!' Hope called down the corridor after him.

Slowly and with a reluctance she could feel, Andreas turned his arrogant dark head and looked back at her.

Hope snatched in a jagged breath. Her nerves were so fraught that she had to immediately pull in another deeper breath. The terrifying finality and obduracy she saw stamped in Andreas's lean, hard face frightened her to the edge of panic. She saw that she truly had no choices left. She saw that keeping quiet about Elyssa's behaviour was no longer a sustainable stance. It was wrong that she should be afraid to tell the truth, she reflected unhappily. Unfortunately, the truth would be most unwelcome to Andreas. He might well dismiss what she said out of hand and hate her even more for making damaging allegations against his sister. But Hope felt that she should not let that daunting awareness prevent her from speaking out in her own defence. After all, she might never have another opportunity. As that reality sank in on her, as she was finally forced to confront the possibility that she might never see Andreas again, Hope was impelled into sudden speech.

'Let me give you my version of events last night. It was me who walked into a room and saw your sister in a clinch!' she admitted with all the abruptness of severe stress.

Outrage firing his brilliant gaze, his lean features clenching taut with disgust, Andreas fell very still. '*Theos*…don't say another word; stop right there—'

Hope thrust up her chin. 'I can't. Elyssa came after me and swore that I would suffer if I told you what I'd seen—'

'How dare you speak of my sister in such a way?' Andreas was white with anger below his olive skin.

'I had no intention of telling anybody what I'd seen…to be honest, I just didn't want to be involved,' Hope continued doggedly.

'You've said enough to make me your enemy for life. The Nicolaidis family have honour—each and every one of us and I am proud of that,' Andreas proclaimed in fierce dismissal. 'It is deeply offensive that you should soil Elyssa's reputation in a pointless attempt to rescue your own. Were you a man I would not have stood here and let you talk about my sister like that. Don't take advantage of the fact that you're a woman.'

'You're the one who's been taking advantage!' Hope protested, a floodtide of anger and agony breaking loose inside her because he had immediately dismissed her account of what had happened at the party. 'You've called me a liar and a slut…you're refusing even to listen to my side of the story.'

'What's to listen to? What's to understand?' Andreas demanded, striding back down the corridor and cornering her against the wall outside the bedroom. 'You spread your legs for a pretty blond toy boy!'

'Of course I didn't!' Colour had run like a banner into her cheeks. 'Don't be crude—'

'That's nothing to what I would like to know.' Andreas slammed his hands to the hall on either side of her head, effectively holding her entrapped. Smouldering golden eyes as dangerous as dynamite challenged her. 'Did you do it in *our* bed?'

'It didn't happen!' she cried. 'I wouldn't even look at someone else, never mind—'

'You forget…I *saw* you looking at Campbell last night,' Andreas reminded her darkly.

Hope was trembling with the strength of her emotions. Her spine pushing into the wall, she was forced to tip her face up. 'But I wasn't looking in the way you mean—'

'What does he have that I don't?' Andreas demanded with savage force. 'Is he better in bed?'

'Andreas…' Hope gasped, fierce embarrassment and dismay at the tenor of that blunt question making her full lower lip part from the cupid's bow curve of her upper.

'Is he more inventive? More exciting? Kinky? What did he do that I didn't do? Didn't I satisfy you? Tell me…I have the right to know!' he launched at her, stunning eyes smouldering ferocious gold with dark sexual jealousy and dropping to the luscious pink swell of her mouth.

'There's nothing for you to know!' she cried in despair.

The tension in the atmosphere was electric. At first Hope did not understand its source. There was a warm, heavy feeling low in her tummy, a buzzing vibration of awareness holding her on a dizzy edge. Holding her indeed on the edge of an anticipation that left her mind frighteningly blank.

'And right now...it's *me* you want,' Andreas purred with silken satisfaction, lifting lean brown hands to skim a blunt masculine thumb over the distended buds of her nipples, which were clearly delineated by the thin wrap.

Hope gasped in helpless response and arched her back. Her entire body felt hot and super sensitive. Recognising her own sexual excitement shook her inside out. 'Yes, but—'

'In fact you're begging for it,' Andreas husked, dropping his hands to her hips and mating his passionate mouth to hers with a bold hunger that in its very intensity was overwhelmingly erotic.

Fire snaked sinuous seductive forays through her heated flesh. She melted like honey in sunshine, yielding to the plundering thrust of his tongue and the heady intoxication of her own response. In one powerful movement he lifted her off her feet and carried her into the bedroom. As he brought her down on the bed his mouth was still melded to hers with devouring passion.

Just as swiftly he relinquished his hold on her. Still lost in the fever of her own desire, Hope clung to his shoulders to draw him back to her.

With cool disdain, Andreas detached her arms from him and straightened to his full commanding height. Proud, dark head high, he stared down at her with icy derision. 'It's over. The instant you let Campbell touch you, it was over. I expect my mistress to preserve her affections exclusively for me.'

Her face drained of colour, Hope thrust herself up

into sitting position. 'I'm not and I never was your mistress!'

From the doorway, Andreas vented a sardonic laugh that scored her tender skin like a whiplash. 'Of course you were. What else could you have been to me?'

Hurt far beyond his imagining, Hope blanked him out and stared into space. She could no longer bear to see him. She listened to his steps recede down the corridor, the distant slam of the front door echoing through the apartment. It was over and he was gone and without apparent regret. He could never have cared a button for her, she thought in an agony of mortified pain.

CHAPTER FOUR

FRANTIC to conceal the fact that she had been crying, Hope utilised some eye shadow to draw attention away from her reddened lids. 'Smile…' she instructed her flushed and unhappy reflection and she practised curving her mouth up instead of down at the corners.

It was seven weeks since she had moved into Vanessa's spare room. Her friend had been marvellous in every way but Hope knew that misery made other people uncomfortable. Vanessa had told her that the end of a relationship was the perfect excuse for a week of tears and laments, but that after that point it was time to move on. Ever since that week had ended Hope had been pretending that she was well over Andreas and miles down the road to recovery.

Unhappily, however, she was finding that maintaining that pretence was the most enormous strain. She assumed that stress had caused the further bouts of nausea she had suffered. Mercifully that sickness had petered out the previous month and, apart from a rather embarrassing craving for olives at certain times, she was fine. If she had a problem, it was with her state of mind. For so long Andreas had been the centre of her universe. Now every day stretched in front of her like a wasteland. Determined to keep up her spirits, she had concentrated on developing a new and much improved business plan. She had visited various financial institutions and was doing her utmost to win a business loan. So far, admittedly, she

had not been lucky, but she kept on telling herself
that success lay just round the next corner. In the
meantime, to meet her bills, she was working in a
shop and selling bags at occasional craft fairs.

'Are you sure you don't want any lunch?' Vanessa
called from the kitchen.

Hope emerged from her room. 'No, I grabbed
something earlier,' she fibbed because her friend had
begun to nag her about how little she was eating.

Vanessa, who ate like a horse and never put on an
ounce, strolled into the ultra-modern lounge. In one
hand she held a sandwich the size of a doorstep. 'So,
how did you get on with that bank this morning?'

Hope almost winced. 'The guy said he'd be in
touch but I don't think I'll be holding my breath.'

'Let Ben back your business,' Vanessa urged im-
patiently. 'Your funky handbags are a much better
risk than the racehorses he keeps on buying!'

Hope smiled to show that she was appropriately
grateful for Ben's offer of financial assistance.
However, her smile was a little tense round the edges,
for if being dumped by Andreas had taught her anything it was that caution and common sense should
be heeded. 'I don't think that would be a good idea.'

'Why not? Five different banks have turned down
your loan application,' the redhead reminded her
baldly. 'Ben's got money to burn and he's eager to
help. In your position I wouldn't think twice about
it.'

'Ben's your cousin. You see him from a slightly
different perspective,' Hope murmured gently.

Hope felt that she had learnt the hard way that there
was no such thing as a free lunch. She had lived rent-
free in Andreas's enormous apartment and that had

come back to haunt her. Instead of maintaining total independence, she had allowed herself to be seduced by the concept of pleasing Andreas and had become, in his eyes at least, a 'kept' woman. As a result, Andreas had found it impossible to see her as an equal. Instead he had regarded her as his mistress: an object and a possession rather than a lover whom he respected. Hope now felt that she understood how rich men looked on less financially successful women. At the same time, she was beginning to value Ben's friendship and did not want to muddy the waters by borrowing money from him.

Vanessa grinned. 'Of course. Ben treats me like a mate but he definitely has the hots for you. I think it's great that he's finally getting tired of the party girls and wakening up to the idea of a *real* woman.'

'I don't think Ben feels that way about me.' Hope was emanating embarrassment in visible waves. 'He likes me and, although he shouldn't, he feels a little guilty that Andreas made wrong assumptions about how well we knew each other.'

'Nah…' Vanessa elevated a mocking brow in disagreement. 'Ben's not that nice. He gets a kick out of having rattled Andreas's cage. We both think Andreas has acted like a callous bastard. But Ben also genuinely wants a chance with you—'

'Even if that's true, and I don't think it is…Ben loves to tease people. Well, I'm not in the notion of anything else right now anyway,' Hope fielded awkwardly.

Vanessa fixed exasperated brown eyes on her. 'Ben won't be interested for ever. Andreas isn't coming back, Hope. He's history.'

Hope's creamy skin was pale as milk. 'I know that—'

'I don't think you do. Have you any idea how worried I've been about you? Instead of living in your little world, you should be facing some hard facts—'

'I think I've faced quite a few of those in recent times,' Hope slotted in ruefully, wishing the other woman would just stand back and give her the time to heal.

'But let's recap,' the other woman said with determination. 'Andreas accused you of sleeping with Ben and he wasn't interested in letting you defend yourself—'

'He believed his sister,' Hope countered tightly. 'I can be very hurt about that but I can't hate him for trusting his own flesh and blood.'

'I reckon Andreas was ready for a change and his sister's lies gave him a fast and easy exit.'

Hope thought back to the fierce emotion that Andreas had betrayed at their last encounter and pain squeezed her heart so hard that she could hardly breathe. Had only his ego been stung by the belief that she had betrayed him?

'Take a look at this...' Vanessa settled a newspaper in front of her. It was folded open at the gossip page and a photo of Andreas with a beautiful skinny blonde. Hope felt as if someone had pushed her below the surface of a pool without giving her the chance to first take in a breath.

'I don't want to look at that,' she whispered shakily.

The redhead grimaced. 'I didn't want to do this to you but you've given me no choice. You won't even open the papers I keep on leaving around for you. But you need to know…Andreas is out partying like mad here in London *and* in New York. He's been seen out with a string of gorgeous models and celebrities. He's not grieving, he's not sitting in nights missing you—'

'I get the message…OK?' Hope breathed chokily. 'I didn't expect him to grieve. I doubt if many men grieve over a woman they think slept with some other man and Andreas is too proud.'

'I just want you to know and accept that you've seen the last of him.' Her friend squeezed her arm in a show of affection. 'It'll help you get over him more quickly.'

The doorbell buzzed. Momentarily, Hope shut her eyes: she had been plunged into the most terrifying tide of despair by Vanessa's lack of patience and tact. In what way was the excruciating spectacle of Andreas in the company of a breathtakingly lovely blonde supposed to help her heal?

'I'm Vanessa…isn't it amazing that we've never actually met until now? Hope's not expecting you, is she?' Vanessa was saying in a curiously loud and incredibly cheerful tone from the hall. 'She's only just got out of bed. In fact, she's wrecked and you'll be lucky if she can string two words together in a single sentence. She's been out to dawn every night this week!'

Transfixed by the sound of her friend giving vent to that rolling tide of outrageous lies, Hope lifted her lashes. What she saw paralysed her to the spot: Andreas stood in the doorway. *Andreas isn't coming back…you've seen the last of him.* Shock seemed to bounce her heart inside her, making it a challenge to catch her breath. Feeling the race of her heartbeat, she trembled. The breeze had tousled his cropped black hair. His lean, strong features were bronzed, his gleaming golden eyes veiled but intent. He looked every inch the heartbreaker he was.

'Thank you,' Andreas drawled smoothly as he snapped the door shut in Vanessa's madly inquisitive face.

'I wasn't expecting you,' Hope framed unevenly and she could have winced at the inanity of unnecessarily stating the obvious.

Andreas watched the light catch the faint track left by a tear on her cheek. Although her eyes still had the luminous intensity of turquoises, her familiar happy glow was gone. In response, the razor edge of his cold, aggressive mood mellowed. If she was miserable, it was only what she deserved. If she was missing him, regretting what she had stupidly thrown away, even better. If she were ready to beg for forgiveness, he would enjoy it even more.

Vanessa poked her head round the door that communicated with the kitchen. 'Would you like me to stay, Hope?'

For all the world as though she were a little kid in need of support around the grown-ups, Hope reflected in an agony of mortification. Recognising Andreas's derisive disbelief at that interruption, Hope almost cringed and took immediate action to avoid any further embarrassment. 'No, thanks. Actually, we're going into my room.'

'Don't be silly, there's no need for that! Naturally you can stay in here,' her friend exclaimed in an offended tone while treating Andreas to a sharp and unfriendly appraisal. 'I just thought you might need support.'

'I'm fine.' Mortified as Hope was by Vanessa's behaviour, she was determined to speak to Andreas in private and without fear of being overheard. She pulled open the door that led into the hall. 'This way,' she urged him in a rather harried undertone.

'We could always go and sit in the limo,' Andreas drawled sibilantly, flicking a chilling glance at Hope's friend. An interfering brazen bully, who he could see walked all over Hope in hobnail boots.

'No, really, that's not necessary, ' Hope declared breathlessly.

It was becoming obvious to Andreas that on one score at least Hope had not lied to him: Ben might own the apartment but his cousin, Vanessa Fitzsimmons, did indeed appear to be the current tenant. Of course the flat could still have been regularly used to facilitate Hope's affair with Campbell. Only as time passed and his powerful intellect continued to dwell on and question the few facts at his disposal, Andreas was finding it increasingly hard to credit that a lengthy affair had even taken place.

For a start, Hope had appeared to be her usual sunny self right up until the week before his sister's party. Hope had an honest and open nature and it would be wildly out of character for her to have engaged in long-term serious deception. He found it much easier to believe that she had simply succumbed to temptation that evening. He was also highly suspicious of the fact that the male involved was closely related to her best friend. After all, before he had even met Vanessa, Andreas had guessed that the woman was hostile to his relationship with Hope. Had Ben Campbell been encouraged to target Hope with his attentions? Had Campbell pretended to be a friend to win Hope's trust and wear down her defences? In short, had Hope been set up to fall?

'In here...' Hope pushed open the door of her bedroom and hoped it wasn't in too much of a mess. Why had Andreas come to see her? Even the most vague and far-fetched possibility that Andreas might want her back reduced her mental agility to zero. Her tummy filled with fluttering butterflies of nervous tension.

Andreas studied his surroundings with eyes so keenly intent and precise that after ten seconds he could have accurately enumerated every visible item right down to the tiny corner of the chocolate wrapper protruding from a drawer. His tension dropped several degrees and his vigilance relaxed as he appreciated that there was nothing in the room that suggested even occasional male occupation. In fact the bed was clearly only occupied by one person. One person with a fondness for cuddly toys. He could not credit that any male would willingly share space with the shabby pink rabbit that had survived Hope's childhood.

As Hope stepped away from the door the disturbingly familiar scent of her herbal shampoo flared his nostrils. Her pale silky blonde hair shimmered across her shoulders like a fall of satin. His every physical sense suddenly on full alert, he studied her. Her fabulous hourglass curves looked more pronounced than ever but he assumed his memory was playing tricks on him. Of recent he had been surrounded by some very thin women, he reminded himself absently, while he fought the treacherous buzz of his powerful sexual arousal. Such comparisons could only make Hope seem more luscious in contour. Regardless, the bountiful swell of her generous breasts below her pink

T-shirt was nothing short of spectacular. His even white teeth gritted.

'Would you like to sit down?' she asked nervously, bending down to scoop a pile of magazines off a chair. Her top rode up a few inches at the back to reveal a slender strip of pale creamy skin.

'No…' His drawl was thickened by his Greek accent and his hands clenched into defensive fists. He wanted to touch that smooth, tantalising stretch of naked flesh in view. In fact he wanted to do a whole hell of a lot more than just touch Hope. After weeks of enduring a worryingly uninterested libido, he was rampant. He wanted to drag her down on the bed, rip off her clothes and have sex with her. Hot and deep and fast, out of control…mind-blowing as it was only with her.

Rigid with the force of the appetite he was containing and the temptation he was resisting with every aggressive fibre of his body, Andreas backed away until she was out of his natural reach. In an effort to control the biting heat of his unsated hunger, he focused on the magazines she had pushed onto the carpet. Evidently she was still obsessively reading interiors magazines. Publications stuffed with photos of period country dwellings groaning with oak beams and crammed with anachronistic kitchens and bathrooms. She was mad about houses. Her nest-building instincts would have terrified a weaker man. Andreas had contrived quite happily to ignore them. But now a taunting, infuriating voice was coming out of nowhere inside his head and asking him why he hadn't given her that fantasy and bought her a country house. Had he given her the opportunity to wallow in chintz

GET FREE BOOKS and a FREE GIFT WHEN YOU PLAY THE...

Lucky 7

Just scratch off the silver box with a coin. Then check below to see the gifts you get!

SLOT MACHINE GAME!

YES! I have scratched off the silver box. Please send me the 2 free Harlequin Presents® books and gift for which I qualify. I understand I am under no obligation to purchase any books, as explained on the back of this card.

306 HDL D359   **106 HDL D36Q**

FIRST NAME	LAST NAME

ADDRESS

APT.#	CITY

STATE/PROV.	ZIP/POSTAL CODE

7	7	7	**Worth TWO FREE BOOKS plus a BONUS Mystery Gift!**
🍒	🍒	🍒	**Worth TWO FREE BOOKS!**
♣	♣	♣	**Worth ONE FREE BOOK!**
🔔	🔔	🍒	**TRY AGAIN!**

www.eHarlequin.com

(H-P-02/05)

The Harlequin Reader Service® — Here's how it works:

Accepting your 2 free books and gift places you under no obligation to buy anything. You may keep the books and gift and return the shipping statement marked "cancel." If you do not cancel, about a month later we'll send you 6 additional books and bill you just $3.80 each in the U.S., or $4.47 each in Canada, plus 25¢ shipping & handling per book and applicable taxes if any.* That's the complete price and — compared to cover prices of $4.50 each in the U.S. and $5.25 each in Canada — it's quite a bargain! You may cancel at any time, but if you choose to continue, every month we'll send you 6 more books, which you may either purchase at the discount price or return to us and cancel your subscription.
*Terms and prices subject to change without notice. Sales tax applicable in N.Y. Canadian residents will be charged applicable provincial taxes and GST. Credit or debit balances in a customer's account(s) may be offset by any other outstanding balance owed by or to the customer.

and walled gardens, he was willing to bet that she would still have been with him.

'Coffee…?' Hope mumbled, her mouth running dry at the high-wire tension in the atmosphere. She could not take her eyes from his extravagantly handsome features.

A tinge of dark colour highlighting his striking high cheekbones, Andreas lowered thick black lashes over his brilliant eyes. 'I won't be here that long.'

'Are you sure? I'd like you to stay,' she heard herself say without any forethought or pride whatsoever. 'A while…' she added jerkily, hoping it made her sound a bit less desperate.

His lashes lifted, revealing his sizzling golden gaze. A combination of sexual desire and fierce resentment held him fast. If he dragged her down on the bed, would she say no? She had never, ever said no to him. Like an executioner letting the guillotine blade fall, he clamped down on that dangerous train of thought.

'I just want to know how you're doing…' Hope flinched, thinking of the blonde in that newspaper photo with all her bones on display. She breathed in hurriedly, afraid that he might already have noticed that her stomach was not as flat as it had been. Once comfort eating had kindly bestowed its largesse in less noticeable amounts on her hips and her breasts, but now visible surplus flesh was creeping onto her middle section as well.

'I've only one reason for being here. I couldn't get in touch any other way,' Andreas asserted with chilling cool, his beautiful mouth compressed with impatience, his defiant libido willed into subjection. 'What happened to your mobile phone?'

'It broke,' she confided.

'The number here is ex-directory,' he pointed out.

'Why did you want to get in touch with me?' Her nerves could no longer stand the suspense of waiting.

'Your brother has left several messages for you on the phone at the apartment. I believe he's visiting London next week. When he couldn't raise you on your mobile phone, he got worried.'

'Jonathan? Oh...' The colour in Hope's cheeks evaporated as severe disappointment claimed her. She felt very foolish and rather humiliated. Andreas had had the most pedestrian of reasons for coming to see her and his visit had no personal dimension whatsoever. But she could not have foreseen the likelihood of her brother suddenly trying to get in touch with her. As a rule she only heard from Jonathan with a card at Christmas and a catch-up phone call after New Year. If Jonathan were visiting London, he would be on a business trip, she thought dully.

'Make sure that you call him. That line has now been disconnected.'

Her brow indented. 'But why?'

'The apartment is for sale.'

That news hit her like a slap in the face. It made everything so dreadfully final. The apartment had been her home for two years. For her, it was still a place full of happy memories. Only now was she forced to acknowledge that she had still cherished secret hopes of returning to live there. She tried and failed to find consolation in the evident fact that at least he wasn't moving some other woman in.

'Don't you still need it?' she prompted tightly.

In silence, Andreas lifted and dropped a broad shoulder in continental dismissal of the topic.

Her turquoise eyes lifted and she noticed the way his gaze was welded to her mouth. Her lips tingled, felt dry. As the tip of her tongue snaked out to provide moisture his golden eyes smouldered and he reached for her in a sudden movement that stripped the breath from her lungs with a startled gasp.

'A-Andreas...?' she stammered, feverishly conscious of the lean, strong hands clamped to her wrists and the scant few inches separating their bodies.

'Don't make yourself cheap trying to turn me on,' Andreas delivered with derisive bite, setting her back from him in a mortifying gesture of rejection and releasing her from his hold.

Hope reeled back in shock from that icy rebuff. Somehow, heaven knew how, the distance between them had narrowed. Had she unconsciously drifted closer to him or was he the one responsible? Whatever, she had never been made to feel more humiliated than she did at that moment. 'You actually *think*...but I wasn't trying to—'

'It's such a waste of your time,' he murmured silkily. 'I'm over you.'

'I *wasn't* trying to turn you on!' Hope persisted, writhing with horror at the charge. Her temper surged up in response to her discomfiture. 'It's ridiculous to accuse me of that. You're the last guy in the world I'd want to make a play for. You're lucky that I'm even willing to still speak to you!'

Dark deep-set eyes gleaming gold, Andreas angled his arrogant head high and loosed a derisive laugh that gave her a shocking desire to kick him. 'And how do you make that out?'

'Well, for a start, you've insulted me beyond any hope of forgiveness. You misjudged me and you dumped me for something I didn't do. The night of that party, I hardly knew Ben Campbell but you refused to listen to me,' she condemned with helpless bitterness. 'When Ben found out what happened between us, he said he was willing to go and speak to you for me—'

Unimpressed, Andreas grimaced. 'How cheap…is he now wishing he had kept his hands off my property?'

'I'm not and I never was your property!' Hope shouted back at him so shrilly and in so much distress that her voice broke. 'Now get out of here!'

Ben had made a grudging offer to speak to Andreas on her behalf but she had decided that dragging the younger man into her personal problems would have been unfair, embarrassing and probably pointless. Andreas's derisive crack about Ben had confirmed Hope's conviction that Ben's intervention would have been unsuccessful. Andreas believed his sister's version of events and would discount any other. He had swallowed his sister's lies hook, line and sinker. Nothing she could do or say would alter that.

'With pleasure,' Andreas spelt out.

As Andreas strode to the door it opened, framing Ben Campbell. 'Are you OK?' he asked Hope, ignoring Andreas.

Tears were dammed up inside her like a threatening floodtide. She thought if she let them out, she might wash both Ben and Andreas away. For the space of a heartbeat, the two men were side by side. With his slighter build, fair hair and fine features, not to mention his trendy jeans, Ben looked boyish next to Andreas, but the concern in his eyes warmed her.

Andreas subjected her to a chilling glance of contempt as if Ben's mere presence was an offence.

'I hate you...' Hope mumbled tautly. 'I've never said that to anyone before...I've never felt this way before either. But what you've done to me and the way you've treated me has changed me.'

'You shouldn't be here upsetting Hope. Leave her alone,' Ben said abruptly.

And the glitter in Andreas's stunning eyes blazed as hot as the heart of a fire. A satisfied smile driving the inflexible hardness from his shapely mouth, he stepped back and hit Ben so hard that the younger man went crashing out into the hall where he fell back against the wall.

'*Theos*...I owed you that,' Andreas growled with seething emphasis, aggression etched into every taut and ready line of his big, powerful body.

'How *could* you do that?' Hope gasped in horror, appalled at his violence and guilty that she should have been the cause of it.

'If I wasn't averse to spilling blood in front of women, I'd kill him,' Andreas intoned without a shred of shame.

Grimacing, Ben hauled himself up out of his slump with a groan. Flushed with anger, he launched himself away from the wall, but before he could attempt to strike a blow in retaliation Hope had stepped between him and Andreas.

'I'm so sorry about this. But please don't sink to *his* level,' Hope begged Ben frantically, terrified that masculine pride would press him into a fight that she was certain he would lose.

'Spoilsport,' Andreas growled between clenched teeth, outraged by the sight of her rushing to protect

the other man, the freezing cool of his innate strong
will icing over the outrage and denying it.

'And to the winner goes the spoils,' Ben countered,
closing his hand over Hope's to anchor her to his side
in a deliberately provocative statement. 'I don't need
to hammer anyone into a pulp to impress her.'

'That is fortunate. You're usually too drunk even
to try,' Andreas riposted with lethal distaste.

Shell-shocked by the amount of bad feeling between the two men, Hope watched Andreas stride out
of the apartment and out of her life all over again. He
did it without a backward glance or a word. She shivered, feeling cold and crushed and bereft.

With a rueful sigh, Ben released Hope's limp
fingers. 'I guess I shouldn't have said that. But
Nicolaidis is an arrogant bastard. I couldn't resist the
urge to give him the wrong impression. He deserves
to think we're together.'

Hope tried to twitch her numb lips into a smile of
agreement. Ben had got punched because of her. Ben
had got punched for being kind and supportive. If he
had chosen to save face by implying that they were
in a relationship, he had only been confirming what
Andreas already believed. Anyway, Hope reflected
wretchedly, what did what Andreas thought matter
any more?

Vanessa had been right. She had been hiding her
head in the sand, living in the past, shrinking from
the challenge of the present. Now she had to face the
future and accept that Andreas was gone for good.
Andreas had moved on. He was seeing other women,
taking advantage of his freedom. A brief, shattering
image of that lean, bronzed body she knew so well
wrapped round that gorgeous blonde in the newspaper

threatened to destroy her self-control. If that image hurt—well, it did hurt; in fact it was a huge hurt that hit her so hard she felt traumatised. But the point was, she had to get used to dealing with that hurt.

'Andreas doesn't care about what I'm doing any more,' Hope muttered, wondering if it was possible to teach herself to fancy Ben. Loads of females found Ben madly attractive and witty. He was around a great deal more than Andreas had ever been. Of course, he did party a little too much and too often and in comparison she was really quite a staid personality. But with some give and take, who knew what might be possible? Perhaps she needed to keep in mind just how many compromises she had made on Andreas's behalf...

When had she ever dreamt of living in the city without a garden and beside busy, noisy roads? When had she dreamt of loving a guy who did not return her love and who made her no promises? A guy who was often abroad and who was so busy even when he was not that she hardly saw him. She might be breaking her heart for Andreas but that did not mean he had been perfect.

He had acted like a Neanderthal if she'd interrupted the business news. He had woken her up for sex at dawn and referred to the candles she had placed round the bath as a fire hazard. He had ignored St Valentine's Day. He had given her a pen that first Christmas. It had been an all-singing all-dancing pen that was solid gold and jewelled and could be used for writing at the bottom of the sea, but it had still been a pen. She had also been left alone while he'd enjoyed the festive season in Greece. Why had it taken her so long to appreciate that Andreas had treated her rather as a married man would treat a mistress?

He had agreed that they could live at the apartment without servants, but had continued to live as though the servants were still invisibly present. He had never been known to pick up a discarded shirt or bath towel. Like a domestic goddess to whom nothing was too much trouble when it came to the man in her life, she had cooked, tidied and laundered. And not once had he noticed, commented or praised. In fact Andreas was so domestically challenged that when she had asked him to make her a cup of tea he had ordered it in. Her eyes were filmed with tears but she told herself it was regret for the two years she had thrown away on such an arrogant specimen of masculinity. He had not deserved her love and it was time she got over him. If she went out with someone else, wouldn't that be the best way to speed up her recovery?

Ben regarded her with lazy aplomb. 'Come down to the cottage with Vanessa this weekend,' he suggested. 'There'll be a crowd. We could have a blast.'

'Just friends?' Hope breathed tautly, tempted by the welcome prospect of being able to escape the city for a couple of days.

'Kissing friends only,' Ben traded teasingly, but there was an edge of seriousness in his tone.

Hope turned a hot pink and embarrassment claimed her. 'Thanks, but no, thanks— I don't know you well enough—'

Before she could turn away, Ben closed a hand over hers. 'I'm not expecting you to sleep with me yet—'

She was really embarrassed. 'No? But—'

'I know my reputation but I'm willing to go slow for you,' Ben promised.

Evading his eyes, Hope nodded. She did not know what to say. She did not think that there was the remotest chance of her *ever* wishing to become that intimate with Ben Campbell or indeed anyone else. Yet, without hesitation, Andreas had slammed shut the door on the past they had shared, she reminded herself doggedly. Presumably Andreas suffered from none of her sensitivities. But then Andreas had never loved her. That was the bottom line that she needed to remember, she told herself painfully. Sitting around alone and feeling sorry for herself would not improve her lot or her spirits. Perhaps if she went through the motions of enjoying herself, enjoyment would begin to come naturally.

The following week, Hope met her brother for dinner at his hotel. More than two years had passed since their last meeting. She was grateful that she had not had the opportunity to mention Andreas during the annual phone calls when Jonathan had brought her up to speed on what was happening in his life. At least she did not now have to announce that she had been dumped, she told herself in consolation. Seeing her brother's fair head across the quiet restaurant, she smiled warmly, wanting to make the most of so rare an occasion.

'You haven't got something to tell me, have you?' Jonathan enquired, arranging his thin features into an exaggerated grimace as he stood up and raising a mocking brow.

'Sorry?' Hope stepped back from him with an uncertain look. 'What's the joke?'

'Well, I suppose it's not that funny.' Her older

brother sighed heavily. 'But when I first saw you
walking towards me, I honestly thought you were
pregnant. Don't you think it's time you went on a
diet?'

Hope reddened with hurt and embarrassment. She
had forgotten just how critical Jonathan could be of
a body image that was not as lean as his own. His
wife, Shona, was a physical education instructor and
the couple and their children led a formidably healthy
lifestyle. Although it had been some time since Hope
had had the courage to approach the bathroom scales,
she was already painfully aware that she had put on
weight and she could have done without her brother's
blunt comments. At present only the larger sizes in
her wardrobe were a comfortable fit. *I thought you
were pregnant.* How could he say that to her? Did
she really look that large? Tears burned the backs of
her eyes.

'You're letting yourself go. It's time for a wake-up
call,' her sibling continued without a shade of discomfiture. 'A good diet and exercise regime would
transform you. Did I tell you that Shona has opened
a fitness salon?'

'No...'

'Business is good, *very* good,' Jonathan asserted
with satisfaction. 'I'll get Shona to send you a copy
of her favourite diet.'

Pregnant. Hope was lost in her own feverish
thoughts. She was thinking of the new bras she had
been forced to buy and considering her tummy's more
rounded profile. She was gaining weight in a pattern
that was different from her own personal norm. Then
there were those secret binges on olives. Hadn't she
once read that some women were afflicted by strange

cravings during pregnancy? But aside of all those vague factors, what had happened to her menstrual cycle in recent months?

'My firm is operating to full capacity. We can hardly keep up with the order book,' her brother informed her cheerfully. 'Life has been very good to Shona and I.'

'I'm happy for you,' Hope mumbled, transfixed by the alarming awareness that she could not recollect when she had last had a period. It was not something she took a note of or indeed looked for or had ever made welcome. But her cycle had always been a regular one. Yet if her memory served her well, her cycle had not been functioning correctly for several months at the very least. Did that mean that there *was* a possibility that she could be pregnant?

'I'll always be grateful that you had the generosity to allow me to inherit mother's estate,' Jonathan added squarely. 'At the time I needed that inheritance and I was able to make excellent use of it.'

It was only with the greatest difficulty that Hope could keep up with the conversation, for anxiety had turned her skin clammy. She was being forced to acknowledge that there was a distinct chance that she could have conceived while she was still with Andreas.

'Hope...' Jonathan prompted.

'Sorry, I'm a bit preoccupied today,' Hope apologised weakly. 'But I was listening. I know you'll have made good use of that money.'

'But it's been on my conscience ever since and it's only fair that you should get the same opportunity. After all, you cared for our mother for a long time and you sacrificed your education and prospects.'

With a look of distinct pride Jonathan laid a cheque down on the table in front of her. 'I can now afford to return the original inheritance to you. If you're still planning to open your own business, a cash injection should help.'

Hope stared down at the cheque open-mouthed and blinked in astonishment. Her sibling had managed to thoroughly disconcert her. Below the level of the table she had splayed her fingers across the soft swell of her stomach while she'd focused on the shattering idea that she could be carrying a baby. But now she had to concentrate on the very large cheque that her brother had just presented her with.

'My goodness…' she said shakily.

'If you're about to embark on a new business, you'll need to be super fit,' Jonathan warned her. 'I still think a diet should be at the very top of your agenda.'

CHAPTER FIVE

ANDREAS saw the artistic photo of the three handbags first. The shot was part of a feature in a Sunday magazine devoted to Vanessa Fitzsimmons's deeply trendy photographic exhibition. There was a miniature silver-on-black Hope label in the seam of the tiny lime-green bag and it was a dead giveaway to Andreas. Courtesy of Vanessa, the handbags had been arranged against a rough stone wall as though they were works of art. His handsome mouth curled. He wondered why he was even looking at such superficial rubbish.

Flipping the page, however, Andreas was wholly entrapped by a shot of Hope sitting on a rock by a river. Several other faces that were far more well known on the social scene featured in the same study, which was called simply 'My friends' but Andreas initially saw only Hope. A multicoloured gypsy-style top open at her creamy throat, her face bathed in golden sunlight and her turquoise eyes luminous, she looked knock-down stunning. A tiny muscle jumped at the corner of his clenched jaw line. His brilliant dark gaze slashed from Hope to the male standing to one side of her: that smug-looking bastard, Campbell, who had a proprietary hand resting on her shoulder.

A boiling tide of rage filled Andreas. He wanted to smash something. Instead he poured himself a drink. It was only ten in the morning. Self-evidently, he was on edge because he had been working too hard for too long, he reasoned grimly. Rage had no place in his disciplined world. All emotion, irrational and otherwise could be controlled, suppressed and ultimately nullified by intelligence. He drained the glass and smashed the crystal tumbler in the Georgian fireplace. The deed was done before he was even aware of his intention.

Hope emerged from the doctor's surgery on rather wobbly legs.

Vanessa leapt up and groaned. 'You *are*, aren't you? I can tell by your face!'

Hope nodded and did not speak until they reached the street. She had been told that she was more than five months pregnant and she was in complete shock. 'The oddest thing is,' she mused helplessly in the fresh air, 'I'm a healthy weight for a pregnant woman. I'm not too heavy. Can you believe that?'

'Andreas Nicolaidis has ruined your life,' her friend lamented in a tone of unconcealed resentment. 'You've just started seeing Ben, you're just about to look for business premises and then it all goes pear-shaped on you. How could you be so careless?'

Hope went pink and cast down her eyes. She had not been careless; Andreas had been, though. Several different types of contraceptive pill had failed to agree with her and Andreas had been concerned that she would be damaging her health if she persisted. For that reason, about nine months earlier, he had said that he would take full responsibility in that field. Unfortunately he had been rather forgetful on at least a couple of occasions that came to mind. Certain methods of birth control could put a breaker on spontaneity and Andreas was a very spontaneous guy, she reflected with a pained stab of recollection.

'So how far along are you?' Vanessa enquired gloomily.

Hope sucked in her tummy guiltily, for she could see that the sight of her changing shape depressed her friend. 'I'll be a mother in just over three months.'

Vanessa stopped dead in the middle of the street and surveyed her in wonderment. 'But you can't be *that* pregnant!'

'I am...'

'But how could you not have noticed?' The redhead gasped, standing back to subject Hope's stomach to a distinctly embarrassing appraisal. 'I mean, give your brother a medal. You *do* look pregnant and yet none of us noticed!'

'I've been wearing loose clothing,' Hope pointed out. 'And people only see what they expect to see.'

When she had first fallen pregnant, her life had been incredibly busy and she had been so wrapped up in Andreas that she had failed to notice that her menstrual cycle had come to a mysterious halt. The other signs of pregnancy had also passed her by. Her health had never given her cause for concern and she had shrugged off the slight nausea and the dizziness she had experienced, believing neither symptom worthy of a visit to the doctor. In more recent months her personal woes had acted like a cocoon that had blinded her to everything outside her own thoughts and feelings, she acknowledged ruefully.

'What are your plans?'

'I have to tell Andreas.'

Vanessa pulled a sour face. 'Let Ben know first.'

But Hope did not fall for that suggestion. For the

first time in two and a half months, she rang Andreas on his mobile phone and left a message on his voicemail asking if she could see him to discuss something important.

It was three hours before he returned her call. 'What is it?' he breathed coldly without any preliminary greeting.

'I need to see you and I can't talk about it on the phone. Where are you?'

Somewhere close by, a woman giggled and muttered something in a low, intimate voice. 'In the UK and busy,' Andreas said dryly.

She squeezed her aching eyes tight shut. She did not want to speak to Andreas and hear his dark, deep drawl and she especially did not want to listen to another woman speaking to him in the teasing tone of a lover. In fact she really could not bear that torment at all.

'I'm also leaving for Athens tomorrow morning,' Andreas informed her coolly. 'This is your one chance to speak to me. Use it or lose it.'

'No, I have to see you in person and in private,' Hope countered tautly. 'I don't think that's such a huge thing to ask.'

'Perhaps not but the prospect is not entertaining,' Andreas fielded, smooth and sharp as a shard of glass cutting into tender skin. 'In short, I don't want to see you.'

'Do you expect me to beg you for five minutes of your time?' Hope demanded painfully, angry, humiliated tears clogging up her throat, for she had not been prepared for that level of bluntness.

'OK. If you're that keen, you'll find me at the gym

tomorrow morning at seven.' He finished the call without another word and left her staring into space.

How was she supposed to tell a guy that cold and unfriendly that she was carrying his child? He was not going to be happy about that. Even when they had still been together, Andreas would not have been happy about that. How much worse would it be to break such shattering news now that they were apart? It had been a long time since they had broken up as well. What male was likely to be even remotely prepared for such an announcement weeks and weeks after the relationship had ended? How could he be so cruel as to demand that she come to the gym where he trained at practically the crack of dawn? He knew the one thing she had always hated was getting out of bed early.

Andreas enjoyed extensive private facilities at an exclusive sports club and visited it several times a week. He had a fitness room at his town house but rarely managed to use it. He had once explained that the club offered him the advantage of sparring with an instructor and training without distractions.

As Hope walked past the limousine in the car park his chauffeur acknowledged her with a polite inclination of his head. What did it matter *where* she was when she made her announcement? she was asking herself ruefully. His office would not have been any more suitable and she would not have felt comfortable at the town house, which he had never invited her to visit even when they had been together. Furthermore, it was foolish to suspect that some slight was inherent in his suggestion that she meet him at his club. After all, Andreas had very little free time and she had to accept the reality that she no longer enjoyed special status in his life.

The weathered older man presiding over Reception asked to see proof of her identity and then told her where to find Andreas. Smoothing damp palms down over the long black wool coat she wore, Hope pushed back the swing door on the gym.

Clad in black boxing shorts and a black vest, Andreas was pounding a speedball with so much energy that he remained unaware of her entrance. She had always been madly curious about exactly what he did at the sports club. Now she remembered him telling her that he had boxed at university. Her attention clung to him. He looked drop-dead gorgeous, she thought helplessly. Every lean, muscular and bronzed line of his long, powerful physique emanated virile masculine strength. She missed looking at him, being with him, touching him, talking to him. She even missed the pleasure of being able to think about him without feeling guilty.

'Andreas…' she croaked.

Although she would have sworn he could not have heard her above the racket of the speedball, his hands dropped down to his sides immediately and he swung round as though his every sense had been primed for her arrival. Veiled dark deep-set eyes with the brilliance of black granite inspected her from below inky, spiky lashes.

It was a bad moment for Andreas. He had picked the club with care. He had thought it an inspired choice of venue where Hope was unlikely to linger or stage an emotional scene. But there she was, garbed in a big black coat and reminding him very much of how she had looked in his overcoat in the barn when they had first met: all silky soft blonde hair and huge bright eyes above that ripe pink unbelievably kissable mouth. That was Ben Campbell's territory now, came the thought, and he went rigid. He hung onto that alienating awareness and welcomed the return of the cold, bitter aggression that slaughtered at source any suggestion of sexual desire.

'So...' Andreas murmured, secure again in his emotion-free zone and cold as a polar winter. 'How can I help you?'

'Well, it's not something you can help me with exactly,' Hope declared in an odd little breathless voice that made her want to wince for herself. Without warning the entire opening speech she had planned to make had vanished from her memory. Her brain now seemed to have all the speed and creative enterprise of a tortoise trapped upside down.

Andreas discovered that like a schoolboy he was picturing her naked below the coat. Angry colour outlined his proud cheekbones and his beautiful mouth curled. He was well rid of her, he decided furiously. He loathed the effect she had on him. 'I haven't got much time here,' he reminded her flatly. 'But maybe you just came here to look at me.'

'No, I came here to tell you something that I find very difficult to say,' Hope advanced jerkily.

'At this hour of the day I'm not in the mood for a guessing game!' Andreas derided and he stripped off the fingerless mitts and flexed long, lean brown fingers.

Hope tried a limp smile. 'Actually I do wish you would guess but it's not the sort of thing you're likely to think of on your own. Although you always look

on the dark side of things, so I suppose that ought to
provide some guidance.'

Exasperated golden eyes lodged to her anxious
face, Andreas murmured dryly, 'What's the matter
with you? You never used to have a problem getting
to the point.'

'That was back when you looked at me as if I was
still a human being instead of a waste of space!' Hope
dared, appalled to find that without even the tiniest
warning her eyes were suddenly ready to overflow
with tears.

Andreas was in the act of pulling on boxing gloves
but he stilled and shot a stern look of gleaming golden
enquiry at her. His stomach had performed a back flip
and he had broken out in a sweat. 'Are you ill? Is
that what you're trying to tell me?'

'No…not, not at all,' she asserted, taken aback by
that dramatic flight of fancy on his part.

Relief washing over him, Andreas dragged in a
long, deep breath to refresh his lungs. He strode towards the leather punchbag. 'Then talk before I run
out of patience,' he urged.

'I'm pregnant.'

Andreas froze two feet away from the punchbag.
Stunned by her declaration, he did not turn his arro-
gant dark head. 'If that's a joke, it's in bad taste and
I'm not laughing.'

'I wouldn't joke about something like that.'

Andreas discovered that he could not make himself
look at her again. He believed he already saw the
whole scenario and what he assumed could only leave
a very nasty taste in his mouth. Bitter anger slashed
through his wall of determined indifference and reserve. Hope had fallen for Campbell. He had come to

terms with that. But that Campbell should have stolen her and used her and ditched her again when she proved to be inconveniently fertile enraged Andreas. He did not trust himself to speak. If he spoke he knew he would make comments that she would consider cruel and wounding and that those words would ultimately prove to be of no profit or consolation to either of them.

How the hell could she have been so stupid? Hadn't she learned anything while she was with him? Of course, she had been able to trust him to look after her, Andreas reflected grimly. She had not had to look out for herself. That was just as well because, in his considered opinion, when shorn of his protective care she had all the survival power of a goldfish swimming with piranhas. She gave her trust indiscriminately. But Campbell had been a very poor bet. He was a spoilt and immature playboy with too much money and no sense of responsibility.

Was it so surprising that Hope should have come back to him for support? What did she want from him? Or expect? Advice? It would be very biased. Money? Suddenly, Andreas was grateful that she was fully covered by her coat. He did not wish to see the physical evidence of her pregnancy. *Theos*...she had another man's baby inside her womb! The very concept of that filled him with antipathy and another even more powerful reaction that he flatly refused to acknowledge. Out of disgust and denial rose rage and frustration. An image of Campbell and his pretty-boy looks before him, Andreas pounded the leather punchbag with fists that had the impact of blows from a sledgehammer.

Paralysed to the spot ten feet away, Hope surveyed

Andreas with a sinking heart. He was furious and fighting it to stay in control. He was saying nothing because he was too clever to risk saying the wrong thing. She watched him fall back from the punchbag and pull off and discard the boxing gloves. Raking blunt fingers through his short damp black hair, he swore half under his breath and peeled off his sports vest to let the air cool his overheated skin.

'I need a shower,' he breathed grittily. 'Come on.'

He wanted her to accompany him to the shower? Hope would have gone anywhere he asked her to go. Even in such tense circumstances it felt amazing to be with Andreas again. There was an electric buzz in the air. As she preceded him into a luxurious changing area flanked by a walk-in wet room for showering, she was as nervous as a kitten.

'Aren't you going to say anything at all?' she prompted tautly, disconcerted that he should be dealing with her news so much more calmly than she had expected.

Scorching golden eyes lit on her squarely for the first time in several minutes. The burn of his ferocious anger needed no words. Her mouth running dry, she tried and failed to swallow. Hurriedly she tore her gaze from the condemnation in his.

'I know you have to be very surprised. I was too,' she muttered, unable to stifle her need to fill every silent, tension-filled moment with chatter. 'But I'm trying to view this development in a positive light—'

'What else?' Andreas ground out in a disturbingly abrupt interruption.

Hope fixed strained turquoise eyes on his lean, darkly handsome features. 'This baby was obviously meant to be.'

'That's a hellish sentiment to throw in my teeth!' Andreas raked at her, his Greek accent so thick she could hardly distinguish the individual words.

Aghast, Hope fell silent. He bent down and extracted a bottle of water from the mini fridge, wrenched off the lid and tipped it up. He drank thirstily, the strong muscles in his brown throat working. As he wiped his mouth dry again she could not help noticing that his hand was not steady. He was, she registered with a piercing sense of love and empathy, as on edge as she was.

'Maybe I should go,' she mumbled. 'I've said what I came to say and I'm sure you must want to think it over in private.'

'I didn't intend to raise my voice. Sit down,' Andreas instructed, grimly acknowledging that the last thing he wanted was to be left alone with the bombshell she had dropped on him.

'I should leave you to have your shower,' she said uncomfortably.

'Sit down,' Andreas repeated, striding past her to snap shut the lock on the door. His reaction to her suggestion that she depart was instinctive. *'Please...'*

Soothed by the rare sound of that word, Hope became a little less tense. 'It's warm in here,' she remarked and began to unbutton her coat.

'Keep your coat on!' Andreas growled as if she had threatened to strip naked, parade around and make a dreadful exhibition of herself.

Andreas decided that an ice-cold shower would settle his tension. He felt as if he were hanging onto his usual cool by a single finger. She was carrying a child and an honourable man did not lose his temper with

a woman in that condition. 'Give me five minutes and
then you can have my full attention.'

Hope sat down in her coat. She was overheating
but in infinitely better spirits: he had locked the door
to keep her with him. She had understood that gesture
just as she understood that he needed some time to
consider what she had told him. She was well aware
that he did not like the unexpected. He liked everything cut and dried and organised. He had never, ever
mentioned children to her. It was perfectly possible
that he disliked children. Some people did. And even
if he did not dislike children, he might still want nothing to do with her baby. He might ask her to consider
adoption. He had the right to make his own views
known and she had to accept that she might not like
what she was about to hear, she told herself firmly.

Andreas stripped off his boxing shorts and strolled
into the shower. Hope stared and reddened and
glanced away and then glanced back again in a covert
but mesmerised appraisal. He was incredibly male
and from his wide shoulders, magnificent hair-
roughened chest to his lean hips and long, powerful
thighs he was quite divinely well built. She had always loved to look at him. But she knew she no
longer had the right to do so and that his complete
lack of inhibition in the current climate merely em-
phasised how shattered he was by the news of her
pregnancy. Her eyes ached and burned and she
averted her gaze from him while he towelled himself
dry with unselfconscious grace. She was remembering
how happy she had once been and appreciating how
desperately fragile and fleeting happiness could be.

Andreas dressed with speed and dexterity in a dark
blue suit. Exquisitely tailored to a superb fit on his

lean, powerful frame, it was very fashionable in style. He looked sleek and rich and gorgeous and distinctly intimidating.

'Tell me…what do you want from me?' he asked softly, opening the door and standing back with innate good manners to allow her to leave first.

Her brow indented, her tension climbing again. 'I don't want anything. I have no expectations. I just knew I had to tell you.'

His beautiful stubborn mouth quirked. 'Thank you for that consideration at least. I would not have liked to find out from someone else. How did Campbell react?'

'Ben?' Hope repeated in surprise, struggling to keep up with his long stride as they crossed the foyer. 'He doesn't know yet. I don't know what I'll say—'

Ebony brows pleating, Andreas stared down at her with incisive dark golden eyes. 'You chose to tell me…*first*?'

'Who else? I mean…strictly speaking, what's Ben got to do with this?' Hope asked uncomfortably.

'He is the father of your baby,' Andreas drawled flatly.

On the steps outside, Hope came to a sudden halt and stared up at him. As that most revealing statement sank in on her she stiffened in appalled disbelief. 'My goodness, is that what you think? That Ben is the father? Oh, that's too much altogether!' she exclaimed angrily. 'How dare you assume that? How blasted dare you? I'm very sorry to disappoint you but you are the man who is responsible!'

Andreas vented a rough, incredulous laugh, for he could not believe what she was now telling him. 'You've got to be kidding…is that why you had to see me? You think you can pin this baby on me? What would prove to be the longest pregnancy on record? I dumped you months ago!'

By the time he had finished making that derogatory and insulting speech, Hope was pale as snow. But shocked though she was, she was also furious. 'I've no intention of lowering myself to the level of arguing with you and particularly not in a public place!' she hissed in a fierce undertone he had never heard her employ before. 'I've done my duty: I've told you. I will not tolerate your offensive personal comments—'

'But what you just said is ridiculous!' Andreas ground out at a lower pitch, closing a domineering hand to her elbow to herd her in the direction of his limousine. 'I assume Campbell has shown his worth in the crisis by bolting. But accusing me in his stead is not a win-win tactic.'

In a passionate temper new to her experience, Hope slapped his hand away from her arm and backed off several steps. 'I'm ashamed I ever loved you and you can stop being so superior about Ben—'

His stunning golden eyes were blazing. 'Get a grip on yourself.'

'At least Ben didn't try to seduce me before we even got out on a first date! At least he's looking for a girlfriend, not a mistress…you know something?' Hope demanded shrilly. 'I wish this was Ben's baby because I bet he'd be a lot nicer about it than you're capable of being!'

'Hope…' Andreas grated from behind her as she stalked away.

'Leave me alone…just stay away from me!' she launched back over her shoulder, not even caring about the fact that her raised voice and distress had attracted attention.

CHAPTER SIX

FOR the second time in as many months, Andreas made a last-minute change to his plans and turned back from the airport.

He did not feel that he had a choice: Hope was seriously distressed. In fact she seemed to be coming apart at the seams. She had slapped out at him, lost her temper and shouted at him, and she had done all of that in front of an audience of interested by standers. It was as though she had had a personality transplant. Yet he knew her as a kind, gentle and unassuming woman, who was slow to anger and blessed with a cheerful outlook on life. Clearly, Ben Campbell was responsible for the appalling change in Hope. He had destroyed her tranquillity and plunged her into so much misery and confusion that she was making wild accusations.

Of course Campbell was the father of her baby! But evidently, Hope did not want Campbell in that role. It seemed obvious to Andreas that Hope's toy boy had cut and run from the threat of paternity and left her in the lurch. So how was that *his* business? And why was he getting involved? Hope was in trouble and she had approached him for help. Who else did she have to turn to? Why shouldn't he demonstrate that he was more of a man when the chips were down than Campbell would ever be?

Back at Vanessa's apartment, Hope was tumbling a jumble of clothes into a squashy bag and asking feverishly, 'Are you absolutely sure it's OK for me to use your family's cottage?'

'Stop fussing. My mother's in Jersey and my aunt, Ben's mother, is far too grand for the cottage now. At least you'll keep it aired,' Vanessa remarked. 'But is it such a good idea for you to leave London right now?'

'I need peace...I have to think.'

Vanessa gave her a wry look. 'Well, not about what you'll be doing with the baby. You're crazy about babies, so I feel it's fairly likely that you'll be keeping the sprog. This sudden departure from city life, however, feels more like you're running away—'

Hope lifted her head, turquoise eyes defiant at that charge. 'I'll only be at the cottage for a few days. I'm not running away. I just don't want to see Andreas—'

'I don't see him around to bother you. I gather by your attitude that he's not going to be pitching for the Father of the Year award?' Vanessa could not hide her curiosity.

'Not while he thinks Ben fathered my baby—'

'He thinks Ben knocked you up?' the redhead queried in lively astonishment.

'I hate that expression. Please don't use it—'

'Didn't you tell Andreas *how* pregnant you are?'

'No, I didn't stay around to exchange conversation after he had made it clear that he was convinced Ben was the guilty party,' Hope admitted heatedly. 'Oh yes, Andreas also accused me of trying to pin my baby on him because Ben didn't want to know!'

Her friend gave an exaggerated wince. 'When Andreas gets it wrong, he gets it *horribly* wrong.'

Hope threaded a restive hand through the pale blonde strands of hair falling across her brow. 'I tried to understand that he trusted his sister and believed in her. I tried to be fair to him but I don't feel like being understanding any more,' she confessed in a driven rush. 'I've put up with enough. I thought that Andreas had a right to know about the baby but now I wish I had stayed away from him.'

'I have a confession to make.' Vanessa stretched her mouth into a wry look of appeal. 'I told Ben about the baby...I know, I know, it wasn't my business. Unfortunately I let something slip accidentally over lunch and when he picked up on it, I couldn't lie, could I?'

'No...you couldn't lie.' But Hope guessed that Vanessa had quite deliberately chosen to break the news of her friend's pregnancy to Ben. Had her friend been afraid that, on the spur of the moment, Ben might say something hurtful? Or had Vanessa decided that it was unfair that Ben should be left in ignorance while Andreas was put in the picture? Whatever, Vanessa had interfered and perhaps she shouldn't have done. At that moment, however, Hope was guiltily grateful not to be faced with the embarrassing prospect of having to tell Ben that she was expecting Andreas's child. Informing Andreas had been upsetting enough. Yet Ben, whom she had been seeing for just three short weeks, was entitled to hear the same announcement.

'Ben was gobsmacked.' Vanessa heaved a sigh and jerked a slim shoulder. 'He's keen on you but I don't think he has a clue how to deal with this situation.'

'I'm not stupid. I'm not expecting Ben to deal with it and stay around.' Hope forced a laugh at the very idea. 'What guy would?'

Vanessa reflected on that question. 'A very special

one,' she said finally. 'But I'm not sure Ben is up for the challenge.'

'Why on earth should he be? Within another month at most I'll be a dead ringer for a barrel in shape!' Hope quipped.

The doorbell went.

Both women stilled.

'It's probably for you,' her friend forecast.

Hope finished zipping her bag and then, tilting her chin, she went to answer the bell.

Andreas levelled steady dark golden eyes on her. 'Invite me in.'

'No.'

Andreas angled his handsome dark head to one side. 'Why not? Is your watchdog home?'

'That's no way to refer to my best friend.'

'Are you saying she has never maligned me?' Andreas fielded with lethal effect.

Hope flushed to the roots of her hair and deemed it wisest to say nothing. But she did very nearly confide that she had always warmly defended him from every hint of criticism. Only now she felt ashamed rather than proud of her once-unswerving loyalty. After all, that very day she had been forced to appreciate that Andreas had never had a similar level of faith in her. He found it easy to accept that she had done all sorts of unforgivable things, didn't he?

He believed she had slept with Ben and carried on an affair with the other man behind his back. He believed she had lied about her infidelity and engaged in all the deceits that would have been required to conceal that betrayal. He believed she had made up a nasty, sordid story about his sister, Elyssa, in an effort to save her own skin. He also believed that, having found herself in the family way, she had been desperate enough and foolish enough to try and lie about who had put her in that condition in the first place.

Injured pride and deep pain warred inside Hope and produced anger. 'Andreas...I don't see any point in you being here. I've nothing more to say to you.'

'You approached me first.'

'Yes and I said what I had to say.' Her heart-shaped face pale with strain, Hope folded her arms in a jerky movement.

'But I've barely got warmed up,' Andreas fenced, leaning into the apartment to call, 'Vanessa?'

Startled, Hope exclaimed, 'Why are you—?'

Her friend strolled out to the hall.

'I was convinced you would not be far. Hope and I are going out—'

'No, we're not. I have a train to catch,' Hope protested.

'I should be in Athens right now and you screwed it up for me,' Andreas delivered, lean, strong face taut with fortitude.

Hope was laced with equal determination. 'I'm not going anywhere with you. I'm not even speaking to you—'

'That's not a problem,' Andreas drawled, smooth as silk. 'I'm perfectly happy to do all the talking. I enjoy it when people just listen to me.'

'I'd know that without even hearing you,' Vanessa chipped in.

If her friend had been hoping to put Andreas out of countenance, she had misjudged her man. Ablaze with confidence and purpose, Andreas vented an appreciative laugh. 'Good.'

His amusement cut through Hope's sensitive skin

like a knife. That was how much her current crisis meant to Andreas Nicolaidis. He had refused to credit that the baby was his and he didn't really need to care about her predicament. She studied him with helpless intensity. Getting by without him was agony and seeing him only increased her craving to be with him again. She had to get over that.

'I don't want to see you...or have anything to do with you,' Hope breathed unevenly, and she reached forward and slowly, carefully closed the front door in his darkly handsome face.

'I can't believe you just did that!' Vanessa gasped, wide-eyed. 'He's the love of your life and your idol!'

'I need to cultivate better taste. That was the first step and overdue.' Hope retreated back to her bedroom to retrieve her bag. She felt as if she were bleeding to death. She wanted to run out the door and chase after him like a faithful pet. For the very first time she was learning to say no to Andreas and it did not feel good to go against her own nature. In fact it hurt like hell.

Four hours later, she was climbing out of a taxi clutching the key for the picturesque country cottage that belonged to the Fitzsimmons and Campbell families. It lay down a leafy lane and was sheltered by tall, glossy hedges of laurel. Cottage was a bit of a misnomer for a property containing more than half a dozen bedrooms. It was a substantial house.

In the charming bedroom she chose for herself below the overhanging eaves she looked out over the back garden towards the gentle winding river and the open countryside beyond. The silence and the sense of peace were wonderful. Her train had been packed and noisy and she had not initially been able to get a seat. Exhaustion was making her droop.

'Carrying a baby is a tiring business,' the doctor had warned her. 'You have to be sensible and take extra rest if you need it.'

It didn't help that it had been weeks since she had benefited from an unbroken night of sleep. Bad dreams and worries had haunted her. Shedding her clothes where she stood, she pulled on a thin white cotton nightdress and sank between the sheets on the comfortable bed as heavily as a rock settling in silt.

Wakening refreshed the following morning, Hope felt her mood lift in tune with the sunshine filtering through the curtains. It was a beautiful day. She put on a light summer dress, attempted unsuccessfully to suck her tummy in and still breathe, and finally went downstairs to satisfy her ravenous appetite for food. She blessed Vanessa when she found that the fridge already contained a few basic foodstuffs. A local woman acted as caretaker and Vanessa had evidently contacted her.

Hope ate her toast on the sun-drenched terrace beside the river and then allowed herself five olives. She had so many decisions to make. But her friend had been right on one score: whether or not to keep her child was not one of them. She had the lucky advantage of being cushioned by the cash her brother had given her. Only now she was no longer sure of what to do with that money. Perhaps putting it into property might be the wisest move.

Her business plans would have to go on the back burner for a while. Too many new businesses failed. Having a child to care for would change her priorities. She was less keen to take on financial risk. Setting up a viable enterprise to craft handmade bags and employing even a couple of workers would always have been a risky venture. But to set herself such a task with a new baby on the way and single parenthood looming would be downright foolhardy.

Ben arrived when she was working on new ideas for bags, an exercise that never failed to relax her. Lost in creative introspection, she did not hear his car arriving. When she glanced up, she just saw Ben standing at the corner of the house watching her. Thrusting aside her sketch pad, she scrambled up, taut with apprehension. With his fair hair fashionably tousled into spikes and his green eyes usually serious, he had a rakish, boyish attraction, she acknowledged. He wasn't a bad kisser either. Only her heart didn't go bang-bang-bang when she saw him and the almost-sick-with-excitement sensation, which she associated with Andreas, did not happen for her around Ben.

'You didn't need to come down to see me,' she said awkwardly.

'I did.' Ben dug restive hands deep into his pockets. 'You should have been the one to tell me about the baby.'

'Vanessa didn't give me the chance.' Hope sighed. 'This was one of the times when she should've minded her own business. She made me feel like I had no place in your life.' Ben subjected her anxious face to a rueful appraisal. 'I'm not going to pretend that this development hasn't knocked me for six...it *has*. But however this pans out, we'll still be friends.'

Her soft mouth wobbled and she compressed it. But it was no good—her eyes overflowed and, with a sound that veered between a laugh and a sob, she groaned. 'The slightest thing brings tears to my eyes at the minute. It's so embarrassing...please ignore me!'

Ben draped a comforting arm round her shoulders but he did not draw her close as he would have done only days earlier. 'You've had a rough week. Don't be so hard on yourself. Vanessa says that you and Andreas are engaged in major hostilities. That's my fault—'

'How can it possibly be your fault?'

'I could've put him right about us a couple of months back but I didn't see why I should. I wanted a chance with you and if you stayed with your Greek tycoon, I wasn't going to get it. I took advantage. I'm admitting it,' Ben said bluntly. 'But even I draw the line at continuing to muddy the water when you're expecting his kid! That has to be sorted out.'

Ben insisted on taking her down to the medieval pub in the village and treating her to lunch. His unexpected plain common sense had left her conscience uneasy. Her own behaviour seemed less sensible. Feeling horribly hurt and humiliated, she had shut the door in Andreas's face and refused to talk to him. It might have been what Andreas deserved and it might have made her feel less like a doormat, but important issues still had to be resolved. Andreas could not be allowed to retain the impression that Ben might have fathered her child. She was not to blame for the misunderstanding. But for Ben's sake and for the baby's, she needed to keep on trying to ensure that Andreas accepted the truth.

Early evening that same day, Andreas brought the powerful Lamborghini to a throaty halt in front of the thatched cottage.

He had leant on Vanessa until she had buckled and told him where Hope was. Hope might well be in need of a break in which to recoup her energies, but he was not willing to accept that she had to be protected from him. Even though he had missed a family christening in Athens, he was feeling good about what he was doing. In fact he was aware of a general improvement in his mood. That was no surprise to him. When had he ever done anything quite so unselfish? Naturally he was proud of himself. Although Hope had no claim on him and even less right to his consideration, he had set aside his perfectly justifiable anger and understandable distaste to check that she was all right.

Hope clambered out of the bath because she was terrified of falling asleep in the water. Wrapping her streaming body in a velour towel imprinted with zoo animals, she padded back into the bedroom. From the low window there she saw Andreas springing out of an elegant long, low silver car. He hit the knocker on the front door.

'Oh, heck…' Her first glance was into the mirror to note that, yes, her hair was damp and messy and piled on top of her head where it was anchored by a canary-yellow band. And her face was hot pink. And nobody was ever likely to suggest that her figure was enhanced by a bulky towel in primary colours. Was her tummy really *that*…? She flipped sideways and wished she hadn't bothered. Sometimes ignorance could be bliss.

Yet even in profile, Andreas looked stunning, his bold, bronzed features vibrant with dark, intrinsically male beauty. Tall and well built, he emanated powerful energy. Her hand flew up to tug off the band restraining her hair. In a panic, she finger-combed the resulting tangle. The door knocker went a second time. Breathless and reckless as a teenager, terrified he would decide she was out and leave if she did not hurry, she raced down the stairs as though her feet had wings and dragged open the door.

His dark, deep-set gaze narrowed below thick black lashes and roamed from the lush pink cupid's bow of her mouth to the voluptuous creamy swell of her breasts. Not even the sight of a pink elephant marching across the towel could dim Andreas's appreciation of her fabulous shape. His eyes flared to smouldering gold.

Her mouth ran dry. 'How did you find out where I was?'

'Vanessa told me.'

Hope was amazed. 'She…*did*?'

'I said I was concerned about you. That unnerved her. Suddenly she didn't want the responsibility of withholding information from me,' Andreas explained lazily.

'I'm glad…we do need to talk,' Hope conceded quietly, backing towards the stairs. 'If you wait in the sitting room, I'll get dressed.'

'Why bother?' Andreas was tracking her every tiny move with keen male attention.

'Because I'm not wearing enough clothes,' she mumbled uncertainly, finding it incredibly hard to concentrate beneath Andreas's steady appraisal.

'You're not wearing *any*,' Andreas contradicted huskily. 'Do you hear me complaining?'

'Don't talk like that,' she begged, her tension rising because she knew she wanted him to talk like that to her. In fact her protest was a truly appalling lie when she knew that more than anything else in the world at that moment she wanted him to kiss her.

Her retreat from the door had exposed the jacket slung down carelessly across the window seat. Andreas treated the garment to a fulminating scrutiny. His hard jaw line clenched taut. 'Whose jacket is that? Daddy Bear's?'

Disconcerted, Hope followed the path of his eyes. Her fine brows pleated when she saw that Ben, who had departed a couple of hours earlier, had forgotten to take his jacket with him.

'*Hope?*' Andreas prompted icily. 'That's a man's jacket.'

Never in her life until then had Hope been so tempted to tell a lie for the sake of peace. While she was wondering whether an elderly gardener with expensive tastes could be the likely owner of a designer leather jacket, time ran out.

'Is Campbell here?' Andreas slung at her wrathfully. 'Upstairs in the bedroom?'

Hope exploded into emotive speech, 'No, of course not. He's not here but he would have every right to be if he wanted to be! Vanessa may have given me permission to be here but the cottage belongs to her family *and* Ben's.'

Andreas paced forward a step. His lean, strong face was set like stone, his brilliant eyes hard as steel. 'When was Campbell here?'

'That's none of your business,' Hope dared shakily.

His intent gaze flared to a volatile gold. 'You made it my business again. Either you're with him or you're alone. If you're still with him, I want to know about it!'

'I'm not discussing Ben with you. You have no right to ask me these questions—'

'If you're still involved with Campbell, why did you approach me?' Andreas launched at her in raw condemnation.

Hope lifted her head high, turquoise eyes dark with stress. 'This is your baby. It's got nothing to do with Ben, so just leave him out of things—'

'That's a fantasy…I finished with you months ago. How the *hell* could it be my baby?' Andreas thundered at her in fierce frustration.

Hope flinched from the violence flaring like a silent lightning strike in the atmosphere. 'In another week, I'll be six months pregnant. Six months ago I hadn't even met Ben Campbell.'

Andreas had fallen very still. He fixed sceptical eyes on her and stared. 'You can't be six months pregnant.'

'The doctor says that some women…of my build,' she selected with care, 'don't look like they're expecting until the last couple of months.'

His normal healthy colour noticeably absent below his bronzed skin, Andreas coiled his restive hands into powerful fists and half lifted his arms in emphasis. 'There's no way you can be six months pregnant,' he repeated, less stridently it was true, but the repetition of that assurance broke the thin hold she had on her control.

'Isn't there?' Hope gasped, angry pink blooming in her cheeks. 'You could not be more wrong. Furthermore, if it's anyone's fault I'm going to be a mother, it's yours!'

'*Mine?*' Andreas echoed. 'You start telling me this crazy story—'

'What crazy story would that be? You got me pregnant. Who was it who said that *he* would take care of the precautions?' Hope shouted at him in a tempestuous fury of frustration and pain. 'Who assured me that I could safely leave everything to you? And then who didn't bother when it didn't suit him? In the shower, in the middle of the night, on the bathroom floor…that time in the limo…'

A slow, dulled rise of blood below his olive skin demarcated the superb slant of his high cheekbones

'How is it that you took that kind of risk with me? Over and over again? How is it that you then have the cheek to repeatedly insist that some other man must be the father of my child? You've got a very short memory, Andreas—'

'No…I remember that time in the limo,' Andreas breathed thickly, fabulous golden eyes not quite focused, a frown line between his ebony brows as though he were literally looking back through time. 'I had flown in from Oslo…I called you to meet me…that…that was pretty much unforgettable.'

Her small fingers curved like talons into her palms. 'I'm so glad it was memorable enough for you to recall.'

Andreas studied her stomach as covertly as he could. But he could not look away. *His* baby. It could be; it might be. He was in shock. 'Now that you've said how far along this pregnancy is, I can see there's a stronger possibility that the baby is mine.'

'You're so generous,' Hope said in a small, tightly restrained voice.

'I'll still want DNA testing after the child's born,' Andreas assured her, not wishing to seem a pushover while he skimmed his gaze over Ben Campbell's jacket. His stubborn jaw line hardened. He still had to deal with Campbell. He wasn't prepared to accept Campbell's inclusion in any corner of the picture. A miniature Nicolaidis, a son or daughter, his first child, his baby would soon be born. It was amazing how different a slant that put on things.

Pale and stiff, Hope inwardly cringed at the threat of DNA tests. He would take nothing on trust. All over again, she felt hurt and humiliated. 'That's up to you but it won't be necessary.'

'What's the state of play between you and Campbell?'

Hope coloured in embarrassment and compressed her lips. 'Take a guess.'

The inference that her pregnancy had wrecked her affair with Campbell put Andreas on a high. Satisfaction zinged through him in an adrenalin rush. He had to resist the urge to smile in triumph. 'I imagine you don't qualify as ideal playmate material with my baby inside you.'

'Ben doesn't see me in that light. He's a friend—'

'Whereas I never wanted to be your friend,' Andreas incised with a look of unashamed challenge in his clear gaze. 'I wanted you in my arms, by my side and in my bed. I didn't feed you any rubbish lines about friendship.'

'Nor did you mention the fact that you thought of me as your mistress.'

'Labels aren't important.' Andreas angled back his arrogant dark head, refusing to award her the point. 'Many women would be proud to be called my mistress.'

'But you *knew* I wouldn't be proud because you

never once mentioned that word to me until after we broke up,' Hope reminded him doggedly.

Andreas strolled with fluid grace across the hall. 'Don't argue with me. There is no longer any need. For the moment I will accept your word that the child you carry is mine.'

Hope shifted a casual shoulder as if the matter were immaterial to her. However, grudging though his concession was, it was a source of great relief to her.

'Why did it take you so long to realise you were pregnant?' he questioned.

'I didn't pick up on the signs. I had too much else on my mind over the last few months.'

'That's all in the past,' Andreas asserted, gazing down at her. She met dark golden eyes and her tummy turned a somersault in response. The beginnings of a smile chased the ruthless quality from his beautifully sculpted mouth. Her heart began to beat to a very fast tempo.

'You've been very unhappy, *pedhi mou*.'

She nodded in uncertain agreement. She was struggling to drag her attention from him but she was mesmerised by the sexual spell he could cast without even trying. A helpless rush of yearning shimmered through her. It had been so long. Her breasts stirred below the towel, her rosy nipples becoming prominent. An embarrassing ache pulsed between her thighs and her face burned with shamed awareness.

'I like what I do to you,' Andreas confessed huskily. 'But you have very much the same effect on me.'

'Do I?' She gave way then to her weakness and let herself touch him again. Her fingers fluttered up to smooth across a hard, taut masculine cheekbone and then flirted with his luxuriant black hair. The wonderfully familiar scent of him that close intoxicated her. Her legs felt wobbly.

'How could you doubt it?' He bent down and let his warm tongue delve into the moist centre of her mouth and caress the soft underside of her lips. Way down low in her throat a moan escaped. She stretched up on her tiptoes and kissed him back with fervent, eager need. He reached down and lifted her up into his arms and then he took the stairs two at a time.

She let her hands sink into the springy depths of his hair. Joy was dancing through her in a heady tide of celebration. He laid her down on the bed. Her hunger for his touch felt almost unbearable. He stood over her, discarding his jacket and tie, ripping open his shirt while he kicked off his shoes. His impatience thrilled her. She lay there, anticipation a wicked spiral twisting down deep inside her.

'I'm so hot for you,' Andreas growled like a hungry tiger as he came down to her.

She opened her arms wide. He tugged away the towel and she gasped and tried to cover herself again, suddenly remembering that she had rounded up in places she had had no need to fill out and stricken by the fear that he would be repulsed.

'I've died and gone to heaven...' Andreas groaned, settling that concern instantly with his bold masculine appreciation of the lush swell of her breasts.

He uncrossed her arms to bare her for his scrutiny.

'Close your eyes...' she pleaded. 'I've expanded.'

'Gloriously,' Andreas declared raggedly, scorching golden eyes glittering with admiration. 'You look like a pagan goddess...very, very sexy.'

Her spine arched a little. He used his thumbs on

the tender crests of her breasts and followed with the sweet, erotic torment of his expert mouth. She whimpered, her hips shifting on the mattress.

'I didn't think to ask...' Andreas stared down at her, taut with sudden anxiety. 'Can I? Is it safe to make love?'

'It's OK...it's no problem...oh, I want you so much,' she gasped.

He traced the swollen, sensitive heart of her femininity and she jerked and writhed, losing control as the exquisite sensations came quicker and faster. The most devastating need had taken her over. She was liquid as honey heated to boiling point. He was a fantastic lover and he had primed every sensitised inch of her to the peak of sensual torment. Suddenly he was kissing her again in a deep, wild, drugging melding of their mouths that excited her beyond bearing.

'Please...please...' she cried.

He told her in Greek how much he needed her, his hands spread to cup her face. Lean, strong face stamped with desire and an intensity that was new to her, he tipped her back. 'I'll be very gentle.'

Slow and sure, he thrust into her hot, damp core, taking her by aching degrees. He stretched her and possessed her with long, hard strokes that drove her out of her mind with incredible pleasure. The tight sensation welling at the heart of her sent her excitement racing higher and higher. The surge of ecstasy she experienced plunged her into sobbing abandonment. It took a long time for the pulsing waves of delight to drain from her languorous body. Full of joy at the wonder of being with him again, she felt her eyes flood with tears and she kept her head buried in his shoulder. But she succumbed to the temptation of pressing tiny little kisses against his damp, bronzed skin, tickling him and making him laugh.

Grinning, Andreas closed both arms round her and breathed in the fresh herbal scent of her hair, revelling in the return of the harmony and satisfaction that had eluded him for months. He smoothed possessive hands over the smooth, soft curves of her highly feminine derrière. He wondered if it would seem uncool and if she would be offended if he examined the tantalising swell of her formerly flat stomach. He decided not to chance it and dropped a kiss down on the crown of her head. The unwelcome recollection of Ben Campbell's jacket slunk into his mind like a depth charge from the deep.

Had she slept with Campbell in the same bed? What do you think, Andreas? A snide, cynical inner voice mocked. Don't the guy's relatives part-own the property? His sleek muscles drew taut. Suddenly a tidal wave of doubts and unease was assailing him. How could he ever trust her again? All men were vulnerable to false paternity claims. Even if DNA testing were to prove the child was not his, wouldn't she still be able to plead that she had made a genuine error? After all, how could she know for sure that it was his baby? At best she was probably hoping like mad that it was his. The last thing she was likely to do was admit anything that might reawaken his worst suspicions.

In the course of seconds his mood had dive-bombed from the heights to subterranean-cellar level. He had dragged her off to bed as if the past few months could be wiped out. But the bitter memory of betrayal remained. Could he really be contemplating the concept of forgiving her? How could he ever forgive her for what she had done? He knew there were sad guys who did do stuff like that. Sad, weak men who let their even sadder dependency on a lying, deceitful woman overpower their brains and their pride. But he wasn't one of those guys. His only weakness around her was lust, Andreas reasoned. That was sex, though; that was allowable. He would sleep with her as and when he liked. That was harmless. But forgiveness was impossible.

'If you pack now, I'll take you back to London with me,' Andreas murmured flatly, hauling his long, powerful frame up against the pillows while at the same time shifting her off him onto the mattress. 'The apartment already has a buyer. I'll have to find you somewhere else to live.'

His cool detachment was as shocking to Hope as a bucket of icy water drenching her overheated skin. He had cut short the affectionate aftermath of their intimacy, Hope registered with a stark sense of panic and loss. Had she really believed that a nightmare could be eradicated and their former relationship reinstated? Why on earth had she fallen back into bed with him again? After all, she was now painfully aware of the deficiencies of what she had once mistakenly seen as a wonderfully happy relationship. Would she really sink so low as to accept being his mistress?

'I'm not that fussed about diamonds,' Hope pronounced grittily.

Halfway out of bed, for he was determined to remove Hope from her present accommodation as fast as he possibly could, Andreas stilled with a frown. 'Say that again?'

Hope shot him a pained glance. 'A mistress is supposed to have diamonds but I don't want any. I *never* wanted any.'

Andreas deemed silence the best response to those incomprehensible statements. Nor did he see it as the best moment in which to confess that some of the charms on her bracelet were ornamented with diamonds of the very highest quality.

'You never ate a grain of food in that apartment that I did not pay for...does that make you a kept man?' Hope enquired curtly.

Stark naked, Andreas swung back at that facetious question. 'What's that supposed to mean?'

'I bought all the food. My small contribution to our shared life,' Hope informed him, her turquoise eyes overbright. 'But you thought you had bought me.'

'No, I never thought that.' Andreas frowned. '*Did* you buy the food? I had no idea—'

'I wish I'd poisoned you when I got the chance!' Hope hissed and, grabbing up her nightdress, she pulled it over her head, leapt off the bed and vanished into the *en suite*.

Andreas listened to the bolt shooting home on the other side of the door and swore under his breath while looking heavenward in vague hope of divine intervention. She had seemed perfectly happy, but he was learning that he could no longer depend on that superficial calm. She could fly from apparent tranquillity to screeching fury with him now in the space of seconds. Was that his fault? Campbell's fault? Was she only back with him because Campbell had rejected her? He could not afford to take anything for granted this time around, he reminded himself harshly.

Hope could not bear to meet her own anguished eyes in the vanity mirror. She had acted like a slut and his coolness afterwards had ensured that she felt like one too. She really hated herself. As long as she behaved like that she would never win his respect. Once again she had been too easy. How could Andreas have sunk so low as to take advantage of her again? And how could she have allowed that to happen?

She had to forget that she loved Andreas. Her baby should be her only priority now. She should never, ever have got back into bed with him again. All that was likely to do was complicate things. Andreas still believed she had slept with Ben. No affair with Andreas had the faintest hope of a promising future. He would not make any commitment to her. Such a relationship would be doomed to failure and their child would also suffer in that breakdown. Sleeping with Andreas had been a serious mistake, but it was not a mistake she had to go on repeating, was it?

Hope emerged from the *en suite*.

Fully dressed, only his tousled black hair revealing that he had not spent the last hour in the average business meeting, Andreas surveyed her. 'All I want to do is take you out of here and back to London where you belong.'

'But I don't belong there. I always preferred the country and that's where I'd like to live if I get the chance. Look...' Hope shifted an awkward hand, inhibited by the need to conceal her true emotions from him with a show of indifference. 'We slept together and we shouldn't have. I regret it very much.'

'You didn't regret it while you were doing it, *pedhi*

mou,' Andreas spelt out with dangerous bite. 'So, what's changed?'

'I'm trying to be sensible for the baby's benefit. I don't want to be your mistress and I don't think you're facing how complicated things could get with a child in the midst of it all.'

Andreas pinned smouldering golden eyes of censure on her and proved that he was not listening. 'This is about Campbell, isn't it?'

Hope winced, for with that one question he fulfilled her every fear. 'It's not even me you want—'

'What on earth is that supposed to mean?'

'I think you just want to take me away from Ben to prove that you can do it. And, yes, you *can* do it. I'm no good at saying no to you...but that doesn't mean I don't know how dangerous you are to my peace of mind,' she confessed gruffly.

Andreas dealt her a look of stark and savage impatience. 'This is all nonsense. You fell into my arms...you came back to me—'

'No...I had sex with you,' Hope rephrased in a mortified undertone, her face reddening as she pushed out that contradiction.

Andreas studied her in angry disbelief. 'Don't be coarse—'

'You had sex with me. Are you saying that meant anything special to you?' Hope was striving not to look hopeful.

Put on the spot, Andreas refused to yield. His stubborn mouth firmed. 'I'm not saying anything right now. It's too soon.'

Unbearable sadness welled up inside Hope. 'We don't have any kind of a future.'

'If that baby is mine, you'll have a role to play in

my life for years to come,' Andreas pointed out impressively.

'A backstage role that you define: a convenient mistress. I don't want my baby to grow up and despise me. If there's a chance that I could be the main event in some guy's life...I want to be free to take that chance,' Hope answered shakily. 'And if I end up alone, so be it. I'll take that risk.'

That was the definitive moment that Andreas appreciated that she had raised the stakes, changed the game, if game it was, and altered the rules without telling him. Either he offered her more or he walked away. He had never surrendered to blackmail in his life. Outrage slivered through him as he angled a brooding glance at the tumbled bed. Just two years ago Hope had been a clueless virgin. But this evening she had had rampant sex with him and then announced that she intended to keep her options open in case some other man presented her with a better deal. For some other man, read Ben Campbell, Andreas reflected in volcanic fury.

'Please say you understand,' Hope muttered tautly. 'I want to try to be the best mother I can be—'

'Naturally. If your child is mine, I'm willing to acknowledge the blood tie and accept a parental role.' Andreas refused to think about how the advent of an illegitimate Nicolaidis heir or heiress would strike the more elderly of his conservative Greek family. 'I will also cover all your expenses and settle money on both of you so that your future is secure. Those arrangements would be separate from any more intimate bonds we shared.'

Hope was very pale and her strained eyes lowered

from his to hide her pain. 'I'm not talking about money, Andreas.'

'I didn't suppose you were,' he drawled flatly, his brilliant gaze cold and level, his handsome mouth set in a hard line. 'But financial security is the most I intend to put on the table. I have no plans to marry you. Not now, not ever.'

She hadn't been talking about marriage either. She had been hoping for some verbal acknowledgement of reconciliation between them and the hint that a degree of caring and commitment could exist in the future. But he was not even prepared to concede the possibility that over time something deeper might develop.

'I wasn't referring to marriage. There are options which go beyond mistress and don't stretch as far as matrimony,' Hope framed with weary dignity. 'Please don't be offended but I'm going to have to ask you to leave. I'm feeling incredibly tired and I'd like to lie down for a while.'

Belatedly noticing her pallor, Andreas descended from his icy tower of reserve at supersonic speed. Concern in his troubled gaze, he strode across the room. With careful hands he scooped her up and rested her down again gently on the bed. 'Let me take you back to London with me. You don't even need to get dressed. I could wrap a blanket round you,' he heard himself suggesting.

'Don't fuss. I'm too tired to go anywhere,' she muttered sleepily.

'*Theos*...I think I should get a doctor to check you over,' Andreas continued.

'Don't be daft. I'm only pregnant,' she mumbled soothingly, heavy eyelids already drooping.

Andreas had always admired Hope's robust good health. She was never sick. Any condition capable of flattening her to a bed before nine in the evening was the equivalent of a serious illness in Andreas's book. She looked exhausted and the translucence of her skin lent her a disturbingly fragile air. Guilt threatened to swallow him alive. He tugged the bedding up over her and tucked her in as she slid over onto her side. He had subjected her to a great deal of stress. That had to stop right now.

He shouldn't be throwing Ben Campbell up and upsetting her either. But had he been a substitute for Campbell in the bedroom this evening? he wondered rawly. Understandably, Campbell had backed off once he'd realised Hope was carrying Andreas's child. That would have been a distinct turn-off for the other man. Was the fact that Andreas had been a substitute the reason why Hope had referred to their recent physical encounter as being just sex?

His mobile phone vibrated. He walked out to the landing and pulled across the door before answering it.

'Where are you?' Elyssa demanded stridently. 'You've got to come and sort Finlay out!'

Andreas raised a wry ebony brow and said nothing. He had never made the mistake of interfering between his sister and her husband. Elyssa was volatile and could be quite a handful. Finlay might worship the ground his beautiful wife walked on but he was no pushover.

'This is serious!' his sister gasped and an uncharacteristic sob broke up her voice. 'Finlay says he's leaving me!'

Switching off his phone a couple of minutes later,

a grim expression stamped on his darkly handsome features, Andreas strode back into the bedroom.

Hope's feathery lashes fluttered up on drowsy turquoise eyes. 'Sorry...did I drift off?'

'Come back to London with me,' Andreas urged forcefully. 'I don't like leaving you here alone.'

With a shake of her blonde head, she burrowed deeper into the pillow. Andreas adjusted the sheet again and resisted an almost overpowering need to just grab her up and stow her in the front of his car. His life had been so smooth when she had just done as he'd asked. Now everything was a battle and he hated it.

He needed an edge. He needed a country house, something Hope would take one look at and fall hopelessly in love with. Cue: listed building of historical interest, oak beams, walled garden, loads of bathrooms. At least it would be a good investment. He contacted a top city estate agent and passed on his requirements.

CHAPTER SEVEN

THE strident call of the phone wakened Hope the following day. In her dream she was wearing a billowing evening frock and drifting gracefully across a vast green lawn towards Andreas, who had never looked more like a movie star. Then all of a sudden the dream turned into a nightmare for Andreas got fed up waiting and walked off. Even though she tried frantically hard to catch up with him, he kept on getting further and further away from her. She sat up with a start and his name on her lips, her heart pounding with panic.

When she snatched up the phone, she somehow assumed that it would be Andreas and was guiltily but deeply disappointed when she realised that the caller was Vanessa. Her friend was so thrilled by the news she had to relate that it was several minutes before Hope grasped what the other woman was talking about. A London fashion designer had seen Vanessa's photographic study of Hope's handbags and, having been hugely impressed by Hope's sense of style, was eager to meet Hope in person and see more of her work.

Hope called the number that Vanessa gave her and agreed to an appointment late that same day. She had to leap out of bed, pack her bag and ring a taxi to take her to the train. Her relaxing country break had lasted less than forty-eight hours. But she was very excited that her designs had attracted the attention of a real trendsetter in the fashion world.

Just before she locked up the cottage, a courier delivered a brand new mobile phone to her courtesy of Andreas. It was her favourite colour of lilac and it was incredibly cute as well as being possessed of every technological development known to man, most of which she would never use, but which Andreas would take the first opportunity to explain and demonstrate in detail. Of course, she knew she shouldn't accept the phone, but she absolutely craved the sense of connection she experienced at the frequent sound of his dark, deep drawl.

Establishing less fraught relations with Andreas made good sense, she reasoned inwardly. After all, they would soon be parents even if they were no longer together. Her throat filled with an immoveable lump. Had she been a little hasty rejecting him the night before? Hurriedly she squashed that weak rebellious thought.

But there was no denying that the tranquillity she had achieved had been slaughtered by Andreas's arrival and consequent departure. She felt bereft and empty and unhappy and that made her so angry with herself. She had to learn to live without Andreas. A positive development on the career front that would also keep her busy had never been more necessary.

Her new phone rang. 'Yes,' she answered all breathless, and on edge.

'It's me…' Andreas imparted unnecessarily, the dark timbre of his sexy voice shimmying down her sensitive spine.

All of a sudden she was reliving the crash-and-burn effect of his gorgeous mouth on hers, his wildness in bed and the complete impossibility of ever replacing him with anyone even human.

'I have some family stuff to deal with this evening.' He sighed with audible regret. 'But I would like to see you tomorrow.'

She breathed in deep and held her breath to prevent herself from saying yes too quickly. 'OK…' she said finally, trailing out the word as if she were still considering the idea.

'I'd appreciate your advice on a house I'm thinking of buying.'

Hope was vaguely surprised that she didn't swoon. Andreas wanted *her* advice? That was a huge compliment. And the advice related to a house? She adored houses. Was he moving? Whatever, it felt marvellous and cosy and confidence-boosting to be approached for an opinion. It was respect…in a small way, she told herself. Suddenly the glitz and the sparkle had returned to her day.

'What right did Finlay have to take Robbie and Tristram to his mother's house?' Elyssa demanded shrilly of Andreas for at least the tenth time.

'You're very upset.' Andreas released his breath in a soundless hiss. 'Perhaps your husband thought he was doing you a favour.'

Finlay often took his sons to their grandmother's with Elyssa's blessing. On this occasion, however, Elyssa was making a drama out of the event. Although Andreas had been at the Southwick home for almost an hour he still had no idea why his sister's husband had left the marital home. Elyssa had been in hysterics when he'd arrived and it had taken Andreas a phenomenal length of time to calm her down.

'Isn't it time you told me why Finlay has walked out?'

'I don't *know* why!' Elyssa slung petulantly.

'There has to be a reason,' Andreas murmured steadily. 'Why are you so afraid that Finlay might have deliberately removed the children from your care?'

'Maybe he's bored with me...maybe he's got someone else. He could be planning to make up insane lies about me in an attempt to gain custody of my boys!' Elyssa cast a sidelong glance at her brother to see how he reacted to that very specific concern on her part.

From the outset, Andreas had been aware that his sister was determined to win every possible atom of his sympathy. Now he grasped that he needed to hear the precise nature of what she termed lies. 'Tell me about the lies,' he encouraged softly.

Her sullen brown eyes flicked warily back to him. 'Finlay had the nerve to imply that I was a neglectful mother just because I left the boys with the nanny overnight.'

'For how long was the nanny left in charge?'

'Only over a few weekends...and once for a week when I went to Paris.'

Reluctant to risk provoking her hysteria again, Andreas struggled to be tactful. 'I understand Finlay's concern. Couldn't you have taken the children with you?'

'I'm only twenty-five years old,' Elyssa responded heatedly. 'Surely I'm entitled to a life of my own?'

'You have a good life,' Andreas told her levelly.

'Now why won't you tell me why your husband has left?'

Elyssa tossed her head. 'I don't want you preaching at me,' she warned him thinly. 'All right... I had an affair.'

Sincerely shocked by that truculent admission, Andreas stiffened. He attempted to keep an open mind. 'Are you in love with this man?'

Her earlier distress apparently forgotten now that she had confessed, Elyssa rolled pained eyes. 'It was only a fling. I can't believe the fuss Finlay is making. As if anyone needs to break up a marriage over a casual affair!'

'I would if you were my wife,' Andreas responded without hesitation.

'You're Greek...your vote doesn't count. You're angry with me but I need you to *make* Finlay see sense. He has huge respect for you. He'll listen to you.'

Distaste gripped Andreas. He could see no evidence that Elyssa even regretted her infidelity. 'How long did the affair last?'

Elyssa gave him a sulky look. 'I suppose I have to tell you because if I don't Finlay will...there's been more than one affair.'

Andreas surveyed the young woman in front of him with incredulous disdain.

Elyssa pouted. 'I can't help it if men find me irresistible.'

Her vanity even in the face of the damage she had done was deeply offensive to Andreas. Somehow he had overlooked the reality that his once-vulnerable little sister had grown to adulthood and full independence. It was not a good moment to discover that he did not like the woman she had become.

'The night that you threw your housewarming party,' Andreas murmured abruptly as it occurred to him that his sibling was not at all the reliable and truthful witness he had believed her to be, 'you said that you found Hope with Ben Campbell. Was that true?'

Her surprise patent at that unexpected change of subject, Elyssa coloured. 'Why are you asking?'

'That story about Hope was a wind-up, wasn't it?' Determined to get the truth out of his sister, Andreas let a deceptively amused smile curve his handsome mouth.

His sister regarded him uncertainly and then she relaxed when she saw the smile. 'How did you guess?'

At Elyssa's confirmation that she had concocted the tale about Hope, Andreas fell very still. 'Why did you do it?'

'I had to protect myself. She caught me kissing another man. I decided to discredit her before she got the chance to tell anybody what she'd seen.' Elyssa lifted a shoulder in a careless shrug of dismissal.

Cold condemnation was stamped on her brother's lean, hard-boned face. 'I'll never forgive you for hurting her.'

'You tricked me into telling you…' Pale with consternation as that truth sank in, Elyssa started to scramble upright. 'That's not fair!'

'How fair were you to Hope?'

'Surely you didn't expect me to *like* her?' his sister snapped with furious resentment. 'From the minute you met Hope Evans, you had no time for me any

more. You were always with her playing house. Yet
who was she? A vulgar little upstart from nowhere! I
couldn't believe that you would bring a woman like
that to my home and show her off!'

'Your spite turns my stomach,' Andreas breathed
in disgust.

When he emerged from his sister's home, he did
not climb back into the limo. He wanted to walk for
a while in the fresh air. Elyssa's vicious attack on
Hope and the jealousy that had powered her abuse
appalled him. Nothing could excuse his sister's cruel
lies or her complete lack of guilt. How could he have
been so blind to the younger woman's true nature?

Elyssa had always needed to be the centre of attention. From babyhood she had thrown tantrums to
ensure she got what she wanted. Of recent Andreas
had become less patient with her constant demands
and had encouraged her to rely on her husband for
support. Naturally he had wanted to spend more time
with Hope. Once or twice he had wondered why his
sibling had so little apparent interest in his private
life. Now he suspected that Elyssa's resentment had
grown in direct proportion to the longevity of his relationship with Hope. Yet he had failed to notice that
anything was wrong. He had also made the fatal mistake of introducing Hope to his sister. It was *his* fault
that Hope had become the innocent victim of her mal-
ice. How was he supposed to make that up to Hope?

He phoned her five minutes later. 'I have to see
you.'

'Why?' Hope said a little prayer that he would answer that he was missing her.

'Something's happened. I don't feel right about
waiting until tomorrow to discuss it with you,'

Andreas admitted. 'It's late...you could stay the night.'

'At the town house?'

'Yes.'

Hope entered a large tick on the mental scorecard she was running on him. 'That would be OK,' she said as lightly as she could. 'But I couldn't actually stay *with* you...if you know what I mean.'

'I'll send the car to pick you up.'

A manservant ushered her into the elegant hall of the big Georgian terraced house and into an imposing drawing room where Andreas awaited her. He looked very serious and her apprehension shifted up another notch on the scale.

'What's wrong?' she asked immediately.

Andreas read the strain in her clear turquoise eyes and reached for both her hands. 'Stop worrying right now,' he told her firmly. 'I think that what I have to say qualifies as good rather than bad.'

'That's great.' Some of her tension evaporated. Her hands trembled in the grip of his and she tugged them free again. Either she was his mistress or she tried to be a friend, even though he had once told her that he didn't do friendship with women. She could not be a mixture of both and there had to be boundary lines. So this was not the moment when she should be noticing that the dark stubble beginning to shadow his sculpted mouth and hard jaw line made him look outrageously sexy. In fact just thinking that forbidden thought made ready colour warm her complexion.

With a distinct air of concern, Andreas urged her down onto a sofa. 'You look tired.'

Hope decided being pregnant was deeply unsexy. Only three months ago, he would have urged her down onto a sofa solely to take rampant, masculine advantage of her horizontal state. But now he was more keen for her to rest.

'Tonight I found out something that shocked me.' Lean, strong face taut, Andreas launched straight into the confession he knew he had to make. 'As you've probably already worked out, Elyssa has been having affairs with other men. This evening, I also learned that my sister lied when she claimed to have seen you in Ben Campbell's arms at her party.'

Hope closed her eyes and breathed in slow and deep. Relief made her feel dizzy. That part of the nightmare was over: Andreas was finally accepting that she had told him the truth all along. 'I'm glad. I really thought that I was going to have to live with that nonsensical story for ever.'

'I wish I could tell you that Elyssa is very sorry for what she's done. But I'm afraid my sibling appears rather lacking in the conscience department,' Andreas derided harshly. 'Before tonight, I had no idea that Elyssa resented your place in my life.'

'She called me your whore at the party,' Hope mused with a little shiver of reluctant recall.

Andreas groaned, his vexation unconcealed. 'Why didn't you tell me?'

'I knew how fond you were of her and telling tales would only have made her dislike me even more. I suppose that even then I wasn't sure that you would take my word over hers...' Hope worried at her lower lip and let her pent-up breath escape softly. 'Of course, by the end of the evening I found that out for a fact.'

Andreas tensed at that reminder. 'I thought I knew Elyssa inside out but I had idealised her. I wasn't seeing her as she really was…spoilt, selfish, shallow in her affections,' Andreas enumerated with a heavy regret that she could feel. 'OK. I admit it. I didn't want to see those traits in my closest relative—'

'You were proud of her…it was natural that you would want to think only good things about her,' Hope told him gently. 'I don't hold that against you. You had no reason to doubt her word if she hadn't lied to you before.'

Andreas rested his brilliant dark eyes on her heart-shaped face. 'You're being very generous about this.'

'I don't think so. I just want to be fair.'

'I'm sorry I didn't believe you, *pedhi mou*. I don't know where to begin apologising for some of the things I've said or for the way I've treated you,' Andreas admitted with roughened honesty. 'But I was so angry that that whole week is virtually a blank. It was a very unfortunate coincidence that you had indicated your dissatisfaction with our relationship shortly before that party.'

That angle had not occurred to Hope before and she was dismayed that she had not guessed that he would inevitably forge a link between those two apparent events.

Andreas spread lean brown hands, his darkly handsome features clenched taut. 'I thought you weren't happy with me any longer. It made the idea that you had sought consolation with someone else seem much more likely.'

'Yes, I imagine it would have done.' But Hope also felt that, having known her so well, he should at least have cherished some doubt of her guilt. But then she had long since reached her own conclusions as to why he had been so quick to misjudge her and saw no good reason to share those thoughts. 'Well,' she added with a typically warm and soothing smile, 'I'm grateful that you know nothing happened between Ben and I...'

'That night anyway.' Andreas could not silence that qualifier. He was fishing, he knew he was, regardless of his awareness that he had no right to ask her what had happened since then between her and the other man. But he was unable to resist his own powerful need to know.

Tensing below that laser-sharp dark golden appraisal, Hope lowered her uneasy gaze to her linked hands where they rested on her lap. Hot pink was blooming over her cheekbones. It was dreadful but she felt as though every kiss she had exchanged with Ben were written above her head in letters of fire and shame. They had really been very innocent kisses but anything she had shared with Ben ought to remain private. In any case Andreas was not entitled to that sort of information, she reminded herself sternly. After all, could she believe that *he* had behaved in an equally innocent manner with the beautiful, sophisticated women he had been seen out with in recent times? No, she could not credit that. She had lain awake a lot of nights while she'd struggled not to torment herself with agonising images of Andreas making the most of his newfound sexual freedom.

As Andreas watched her fair skin turn pink a cold, heavy sensation settled like concrete in his stomach. He knew how unreasonable he was being but he had very much hoped to hear her say that, challenging though the circumstances had been, she had stayed loyal to him in spite of everything. Intelligence told him that was unlikely. Intelligence told him that blush was as good as a signed confession in triplicate. She had slept with Campbell. Of course she had.

Andreas endeavoured to put the entire controversial subject out of his mind. He was a pragmatic man. What had been done could not be undone. He offered Hope a soft drink, which she declined. He poured a whisky that he drank down in two minimal gulps. Pragmatic though he believed himself to be, he was assailed by another unfortunate reflection: there was no point hoping that at some future stage she would tell him that Campbell had been absolute rubbish in bed. She was not that kind of woman. He would never, ever know whether she compared them.

'I feel that I should make an effort to clear the air,' Hope remarked hesitantly, fixing anxious turquoise eyes on Andreas.

'As regards what…exactly?'

'As regards Ben,' Hope proffered gently.

Andreas froze. His imagination went into a loop. In the name of honesty, she was about to talk like a canary, telling everything right down to the tiniest and most insignificant detail. He wanted to know but feared that knowing would torture him. He breathed in deep. 'Hope…'

'No, please let me say what I want to say first,' Hope interrupted apologetically. 'Ben's been so very kind to me. I want you to understand that he's a much nicer person than people seem to appreciate. I think you'd really like Ben if you got to know him…'

That was the moment when Andreas knew that he should have drunk all the whisky in the decanter in the hope of anaesthetising his sensibilities into a stupor. Hope was engaging in a more refined form of torture than he had even envisaged. She was keen for him to get to know Ben. In the eternally sunny world she inhabited they were probably all destined to become the very closest of mutually supportive friends. There was just one small problem. He could not think of Ben Campbell without wishing to wipe him with maximum violence from the face of the earth.

'I'm fond of Ben and he's been a terrific friend.'

'That's cool,' Andreas breathed between clenched teeth.

'I would like him to stay a friend,' Hope advanced.

Valiantly, Andreas shrugged while conceding that the eating of humble pie was his equivalent of eating rat poison. But he had screwed up badly. She was expecting his baby and he had put her through hell and this was his penance. Presumably, if he agreed with even the most fanciful and unreasonable requests and expectations, all her fears would be soothed and everything would finally go back to normal. Normal. That was his only ambition. 'Why not…?'

Hope wondered why he was so tense. Was he annoyed because she had said earlier that she believed that she ought to sleep alone? The belief was not set in stone. She was open to clever argument and even downright seduction. Had she hurt his feelings with her embargo? His ego? Was that why he was chucking whisky down his throat as if there were no tomorrow? What was wrong? As a rule, he was a very occasional drinker.

'You should go to bed,' Andreas suggested rather abruptly. 'We have an early start in the morning.'

'Oh, my goodness, I never even asked you about the house—'

Andreas opened the door into the hall. 'It'll keep until tomorrow.'

Hope swallowed back a yawn. In truth she was very tired. 'I haven't even told you my own news yet.' She laughed on the way up the imposing stairs. 'Guess what? I've been discovered by the fashion world. I met Leonie Vargas this afternoon and I'm being offered the chance to design bags for her next collection!'

'That's great.' Andreas thought about what he knew about Leonie Vargas. In his conservative opinion, she was a very eccentric lady who wore even stranger outfits. Even so she had become spectacularly rich designing clothes for the young and hip. Hope had really found her niche, Andreas thought with satisfaction and considerable relief. The Vargas woman would probably be delighted with a bag that resembled a tomato. His biggest fear had always been that Hope would meet with the kind of rejection that crushed a vulnerable creative personality.

'See you in the morning...' Hope whispered, hovering within reach.

Andreas resisted temptation. She had taken the trouble to warn him off before she had even agreed to stay. In the light of that prohibition, testing the boundaries would be a bad move. Tomorrow, however, after he had proposed and she had the engagement ring on her finger, he would probably bulldoze down the boundaries. Gently bulldoze, he adjusted, thinking about the baby. In any case he still had one or two arrangements to put in place for the next day.

Hope surveyed the beautifully decorated guest room. She had finally made it into the town house. A barrier had been crossed. But she remained far more aware that she had been carefully kept from the same door for two years.

Since Andreas had dumped her she had learned some hard lessons. Andreas had always viewed her as his mistress, probably still did and was very unlikely to ever see her in any other light. For the moment, her pregnancy had brought down several barriers but she suspected that in time the same barriers would be reinstated. So, although she was horrendously weak where he was concerned and changed like the wind according to the level of his proximity, she needed to be sensible and keep her distance.

When Andreas had told Hope that he wanted her opinion on a house, she had had no real idea what to expect. But she had nonetheless assumed that he would only be interested in a city property within easy reach of his office. Instead she was tucked into a helicopter and informed that their destination lay outside London. Mesmerised by his pronounced air of mystery, she was a really good sport about the fact that the seat belt had to be loosened to fit her.

When the helicopter came in to land at Knightmere Court, Andreas was experiencing the high of a male convinced that he had picked a sure-fire winner. He had picked Knightmere from a selection of six large country properties. It ticked every box on the list of desirable qualities he had drawn up and Hope was already staring out the window with an appropriately transfixed expression pinned to her face.

'My goodness...' Hope exclaimed weakly as he lifted her out of the craft.

Andreas took her on a very brief outside tour just to ensure that she got a tantalising flavour of the extensive grounds, which included a knot and topiary garden, the all-important walled garden and a park as much ornamented by a pedigree flock of sheep as by the trees. He drew her attention variously to the dove-cote, the clock tower and the lake in the distance. He had picked a building that fairly bristled with historic features.

'The estate comes with a considerable amount of land, sufficient to ensure that the superb views will remain unaltered,' Andreas informed her, having read and inwardly digested every packed and detailed page of the glossy sales brochure.

Hope blinked and wondered what was the matter with him. She was not aware that he had ever shown any interest in country life. But his disinterest in his surroundings embraced city living too, she reflected with a slight frown. As long as the luxury comforts, services and privacy he took entirely for granted were available, Andreas was maddeningly indifferent to his home environment. Yet now all of a sudden he sounded rather like an enthusiastic estate agent.

Round the next corner she was treated to her first full view of the south front of the ancient Tudor manor house. 'My goodness...' she said again, utterly charmed by the soft mellow colour of the bricks and the latticed windows sparkling in the sunshine. 'It's beautiful.'

'Indoors you'll have to exercise your imagination,' Andreas remarked, nodding acknowledgement of the discreet older man who appeared at the entrance and spread the door wide for them. 'Knightmere has been empty for more than three years, although it has been extensively renovated.'

'Was it originally owned by one particular family?'

'Yes. The family line died out with an elderly spinster. A foreign businessman bought it but the repairs took longer than expected and he never lived here. He's now moved abroad again and the house is back on the market.'

'Wouldn't this place be too far from the city for you?'

'I'd use the helicopter.'

Her turquoise eyes were perplexed. 'It's just not the sort of property that I would've expected you to be interested in. I thought possibly you were thinking of converting it into a hotel or apartments or something—'

'No.'

'Then if you bought it, this would actually be your home?'

'My country home and where I would spend most of my time...yes,' Andreas confirmed. 'I like space around me.'

'There's certainly plenty of that,' Hope conceded. 'It's a huge house. How many bedrooms are there?'

'A dozen or so.' Andreas shifted a casual shoulder. 'But I have a large family circle. On special occasions those rooms would be easy to fill.'

Hope scanned the panelled walls, massive overhead oak beams and the huge elaborate fireplace, which bore the carved date of a year in the sixteenth century. She was fascinated. 'This must have been the Great Hall. It's so old and yet so wonderfully well preserved,' she whispered in frank awe of her surroundings.

Andreas surveyed her rapt profile and decided it was a done deal; she was reacting exactly as he had hoped. He allowed her to roam where her fancy took her and watched her enchantment grow. No nook and no cranny remained unexplored. An ancient range had been left intact at one end of the vast kitchen and she went into raptures over it and the beautifully carved free-standing units. Inspecting a procession of stream-lined opulent bathrooms almost emptied her of superlative comments.

Andreas walked her back outside through the courtyard. 'Do you think I should buy it?' he asked, confidence riding high.

'Oh, yes...it's fantastic,' Hope murmured dreamily.

Andreas pushed open the cast-iron gate into the walled garden, which was a riot of early summer roses and lush greenery. 'Close your eyes,' he urged softly. 'I have a surprise for you.'

Obediently she let her lashes dip and then lifted them again at his bidding. A traditional canvas canopy screened the sun from the tumbled cushions that were piled invitingly on the elegant striped rug spread across the manicured grass. A wicker hamper sat invitingly open with linen napkins, a chrome wine cooler and crystal glasses already lined up in readiness. It was a picnic Nicolaidis style, she registered in wonderment, so perfect in presentation and backdrop that she felt as if she had wandered into a picture in a magazine. It would no doubt knock her home-made picnics of the past into a cocked hat.

Her generous smile lit up her lovely face. 'Oh, this is a glorious surprise.'

'I wanted to do something special that you'd really appreciate, *pedhi mou*.'

Her mobile phone rang. Wishing that she had thought to switch it off, she dug it out. It was Ben.

Ready embarrassment coloured her cheeks and she half turned away to speak. 'Ben…hi.'

Ben was ringing to congratulate her on the offer she had received from Leonie Vargas.

'Don't mind me,' Andreas breathed very dryly.

'Could I call you back later?' Hope asked Ben in a whisper that sounded to her own ears like a shout. 'I'm so sorry but I can't really chat right now.'

As she put the phone away again the silence fairly bulged with hostile undertones. Andreas was furious. At the optimum wrong moment, Campbell phoned. Was he expected to accept that? Being haunted by the ex-boyfriend? With difficulty he suppressed his annoyance by reminding himself that Hope was friendly with everybody she met.

'Let's eat,' Andreas suggested.

The hamper was packed to the brim with delicious items. Hope sipped fruit juice and ate until she could eat no more. She told him what Leonie Vargas was like in the flesh and made him laugh. Resting back against the tumbled cushions, she relaxed and feasted her eyes on his lean, powerful face.

Andreas stretched out a lean, long-fingered hand to her. 'Come here…' he urged huskily.

A quiver of forbidden excitement tugged at her. After a split second of hesitation, her hand reached out to close into his. He tugged her close, leaning over her to scan her with brilliant golden eyes. 'Let's get married and make Knightmere our home,' he murmured smoothly.

CHAPTER EIGHT

HOPE'S mouth ran dry and shock tore through her tensed body. Andreas had taken her by surprise. She closed her eyes tight against the intrusion of his and let herself savour just for a moment the sheer joy of actually being asked to be his wife. There was nothing she wanted more but she knew that it would not be right for her to say yes unless he said the right words. Unfortunately those same words were words she had long since accepted that she would never hear from him.

'Why?' she questioned tightly. 'Why are you asking me to marry you?'

His ebony brows pleated. 'Isn't that obvious?'

The first twist of disappointment tore at her and she opened strained turquoise eyes. 'You're thinking about the baby.'

'Of course. No Nicolaidis that I know of has ever been born outside the bonds of matrimony,' Andreas informed her with considerable pride.

His reasons for asking her to become his wife were fairly piling up, Hope conceded unhappily. One, she was pregnant. Two, he was keen to respect the conventions.

'It's only two days since you told me that you would *never* marry me,' Hope reminded him very quietly.

'That was when I was still under the impression that you had been unfaithful,' Andreas asserted without discomfiture. 'I think we should go for a quick, quiet ceremony and throw a big party afterwards. What do you think?'

Slowly, Hope withdrew her fingers from his and sat up. 'I think you're not going to like my answer.'

Andreas misunderstood. 'If you prefer a more traditional wedding, I don't mind. Have as many frills as you like. *How* we do it isn't important as long as we do it before the baby's born.'

Hope pushed herself upright. 'I'm afraid the answer has to be…no.'

'*No?*' She saw that it had not once occurred to Andreas that he might meet with rejection.

'I love the house, love the picnic—' Love you too, Hope reflected painfully but kept that admission to herself '—but unfortunately you don't want to marry me for the right reasons.'

Utterly taken aback by that criticism, Andreas sprang upright, dark golden eyes incredulous. 'What are the right reasons?'

'If you don't know, there's no point in me spelling them out for you,' she said heavily.

'Are you still determined to keep your options open? Is that what this is all about?' Andreas ground out.

Her brow indented. 'I don't know what you're getting at.'

'Or are you punishing me for listening to my sister three months ago and letting you down?' Andreas demanded in a raw undertone.

Hope studied him with pained intensity. 'I wouldn't behave like that. But I am afraid that you were so willing to believe Elyssa's lies because you wanted your freedom back—'

'I always had my freedom. I made a free choice to be with you!' Andreas contradicted.

'And when I made the mistake of reminding you that we'd been together almost two years, you were in no mood to celebrate.' Hope sighed. 'There was no question of your making a commitment to me then—'

His even white teeth gritted. 'Everything's changed since then—'

'Yes. But you don't need to put a ring on my wedding finger because I fell pregnant,' Hope told him gently.

'How are you planning to manage without me?'

Hope lost colour at that crack. 'Are you saying that if I don't marry you, you'll break up with me again?'

An electrifying silence fell.

His beautiful dark deep-set eyes struck sparks from hers. 'No, I'm not saying that. I'd have to be a real bastard to abandon the mother of my child in any circumstances.'

'For goodness' sake, I know you're not that.' Hope felt as though she were standing on the edge of a chasm in the middle of an earthquake. If she wasn't careful she might tumble into the chasm and lose everything. Was she being foolish? Should she be willing to settle for a marriage of convenience with a guy who didn't love her? Or was it that she was more scared of Andreas marrying her and then regretting it?

While she was frantically questioning whether or not she was making the biggest mistake of her life, Andreas closed his arms round her. 'I made you happy before...I can do it again,' he intoned fiercely.

'I know, but—'

'*Theos*…Just you try and find this same fire with someone else!' He bent his arrogant dark head and crushed her ripe mouth under his, unleashing a passion that took her by storm. His lips were firm and warm and wonderful on hers and she could not get enough of his kisses.

Breathless and trembling, she knotted her fingers into the shoulders of his jacket to hold him close. She did not want to set him free to find someone else. She did not want to be alone.

'Andreas…?' she framed through reddened lips, turquoise eyes clinging in urgent appeal to his. 'Don't get the wrong idea about what I'm about to say. I'm not suggesting that I be your mistress. But could we live together instead of getting married?'

Andreas was a long way from happy with that proposition. His smoothly laid plans had been derailed when he'd least expected it. He felt hollow, bewildered by his failure, quite unlike himself.

Had he rushed her too much? He always moved fast and made decisions at the speed of the light but she did not. Once, though, she had had touching faith in him and his judgement. Now, however, she was wary, unsure of herself and of him. For the first time he recognised how much he must have hurt her when he'd dumped her. He could hardly blame her for being afraid to trust him again.

He saw that there had been a fatal flaw in his approach. He had put more effort into marketing the house than himself. Having recognised the problem, he saw the solution and came up with a fresh strategy. That disturbing sense of disorientation that had afflicted him mercifully vanished. All he had to do was demonstrate that he would make a perfect husband and a fantastic father.

'Andreas...' Hope prompted worriedly, afraid she had offended him.

The brooding light in his dark reflective gaze ebbed and his slow, charismatic smile curved his handsome mouth. 'I'll buy the house this afternoon. How soon will you move in?'

She blinked, thrown by his immediacy. 'Whenever you like.'

'I like it best when you're not out of my sight for longer than five minutes, *pedhi mou*,' Andreas told her, tugging her up against his lean, powerful frame and anchoring her below one strong arm while he called the agent to negotiate.

'No, you're not to look at that,' Andreas scolded, flipping an offending newspaper out of her reach six weeks later.

'Why not?' Hope watched him lounge back against the crisp white pillows. The sheet had dropped to below his waist, exposing the hard, hair-roughened expanse of his bronzed torso and the sleek, muscular strength of his superbly fit body. He looked breathtakingly handsome.

'There's an entry about us in the gossip column...I don't want you lowering yourself to look at trash like that,' Andreas delivered in a tone of finality.

Unimpressed, Hope put out her hand. 'Give it to me,' she told him.

A raw masculine grin slashed his beautiful mouth. 'No...'

'Stop being bossy!' Levering herself up, Hope flung herself across him in an effort to wrest the paper

from him. Laughing with rich appreciation, he caught
her in his arms and pressed her gently back against
the pillows. Teasing golden eyes met hers. 'Behave
yourself!'

'You can't censor what I read—'

'If there is the tiniest risk that something might
upset you it's my duty to protect you from it. I'm
Greek. You're my woman and I look after you. Learn
to live with what you can't fight,' Andreas warned
with unblemished good humour.

'I'll just walk down to the village and buy another
copy.'

'You're supposed to be taking it easy.' Frowning,
Andreas handed the disputed item over. 'That was
blackmail.'

'I know.' Far from ashamed of herself, Hope wrig-
gled up again, snuggled back into him for support and
opened the paper. Sometimes it was rather sweet to
be treated like impossibly fragile spun glass, but other
times it made her feel horribly like a burden. It was
bad enough that he should be full of energy and vi-
tality while she was falling asleep in the middle of
the day. In addition, anything more intimate than a
hug was off the menu as well. When her cautious
gynaecologist had said that her exhaustion could become a source of concern, Andreas had decided that
sex was absolutely out of the question.

Having leafed through the newspaper, Hope found
a most unflattering photo of herself that seemed to
concentrate rather cruelly on her pregnant stomach.
She looked like a large woman overfilling a little
black dress, an archetypal ship in full sail trundling
across the pavement. The photo had been taken two
days earlier as they'd left the well-known restaurant

where Andreas's grandfather, Kostas, had entertained them to dinner and initially trying questions. She had soon warmed to the blunt-spoken older man, however. Kostas Nicolaidis had made it clear that, although he would much prefer them to marry, he was overjoyed that she was carrying his grandson's baby and that Andreas was finally settling down.

'Oh, no…' Hope exclaimed, aghast, as she started reading the article beside the photo.

'So what's wrong with my grandson that you won't make an honest man of him?' Kostas had asked baldly, and there were those exact same words in print, clearly overheard and passed on to the columnist. Below the execrable title, BAG LADY REFUSES NICOLAIDIS HEIR, virtually every female that Andreas had ever dated was listed, the suggestion being that he had been turned down because no sane female would seek to tie down a rampant womaniser.

'Kostas will be thrilled. He loves to see his name in newsprint,' Andreas commented cheerfully.

'But I look simply *huge*!' she wailed in embarrassment.

Andreas stretched appreciative hands across the rounded swell of her stomach, stretched them just a little more and contrived to link his fingers. 'You look fantastic, really, really pregnant now. Ripe like a peach, *pedhi mou*.'

'Very round and squashy?' Hope refused to be comforted. 'Aren't you angry that everybody knows that you proposed and I said no?'

'You must be kidding.' Andreas laughed off that idea with disconcerting verve.

Her brows pleated, for she had assumed that he

would be furious that something so private had been accidentally brought by his grandfather into the public domain. 'You don't mind?'

'Not in the slightest,' Andreas asserted silkily. 'And when you get to meet the rest of my relatives this weekend you'll understand why. I'm the golden boy because I tried to get a wedding ring on your finger and you'll be—'

'The horrible witch who doesn't appreciate you!' she slotted in, cringing at that new awareness.

'Nonsense. My great-aunts will be very keen to talk me up. You are destined to spend the entire weekend listening to stories that represent me as Mr Wonderful—clean-living, kind to old ladies and animals and stupendous with children. I'll bet you right now that nobody mentions my late father and his three divorces. He's the family skeleton and would give the wrong impression.'

An involuntary gurgle of laughter escaped Hope and she relaxed. The past six weeks had been just about the happiest and busiest of her life. They had managed to move into Knightmere the previous month. Andreas had pulled strings, called in favours and brought in an interior design firm as well as a project manager to ensure that the wonderful old house had been made habitable in the least possible amount of time. A full quota of domestic staff had been hired and Hope had been left with little more to do than design bags.

That had proved to be just as well because pregnancy was slowing her down. Just occasionally her worries got on top of her. Had saying no to the proposal been the right thing to do? He had not mentioned the subject since, which suggested that he was quite content with things as they were. How could a guy so gorgeous cheerfully settle for a woman who was the shape of a very ripe peach? Was it guilt that was making Andreas so perfect? Guilt that he had misjudged her and left her alone for several months?

Perfect was not an exaggeration of his attitude towards her or his behaviour. He had begun working much shorter hours and cutting down on his trips abroad. He had attended all her pre-natal appointments with her. He had read a book on pregnancy with the result that he descended into pure panic if she experienced the slightest twinge of pain in any part of her body. When she'd got a cramp in her leg one evening he had wanted to take her to Casualty and when she'd refused he had sat up all night watching over her. He had also been pleasant to her friend, Vanessa, and had tolerated her receiving regular phone calls from Ben, who had been travelling round Europe for several weeks.

In addition, Andreas had been kind, affectionate, supportive and, as always, wonderfully entertaining. Being sexy came naturally to him so she didn't count that. But although he could well have aspired to sainthood, not one word had Andreas said about love. So there it was, Hope thought heavily. She had to accept that she just did not have what it took to inspire Andreas with love. As long as there was no other woman out there who had the power that she lacked, she supposed she was all right. After all, she loved him and she was living with him and she would soon give birth to his child. Wasn't it rather greedy to want more?

'I have a couple of things I need to deal with at the office before we leave for Greece. I'll meet you at the airport at six,' Andreas murmured above her head, wishing he could take her to the office with him and then frowning in bemusement at the seriously un-cool and embarrassing oddity of that last absent-minded thought.

He assumed that he was always stressing about her because she was pregnant. She was always on his mind. When he was away from her, he found it par-ticularly difficult to concentrate on work. Reading that gruesome book had been a serious error. He had not slept for a couple of nights after it and the worst thing of all had been the necessity of keeping quiet about the concerns that had been awakened by what he had read. He had dumped the book. He didn't want *her* reading scary stuff of that nature.

'Hope…?' Andreas probed.

He tugged her to one side and bent over her. She was fast asleep. He listened to hear her breathing just in case it didn't sound normal. With great care he settled her down on the pillows. He would warn the housekeeper to check on her.

Hope was really annoyed when she realised that she had drifted off and missed Andreas's departure. Having completed her packing the day before, she donned the lilac tunic and cropped trousers she had decided to travel in. Andreas phoned an hour later.

'Make sure you eat some lunch,' he instructed.

'Stop fussing…' She walked over to the window of the room that she used as a design studio. It over-looked the courtyard where a car was pulling up. It was a Porsche and she grinned when she saw a fa-miliar tousled blond head emerging from the driver's seat. 'Oh, my goodness, Ben's here…sorry, I have to go!' she told Andreas in a rush.

In his London office, Andreas stared fixedly down at the phone in his hand. She had been so overjoyed to see Campbell she had ended the call. He endeavoured to return his attention to the report on his desk. Campbell had been out of the country for weeks. Hope seemed to think he simply enjoyed travel but Andreas suspected that Ben had gone abroad in an effort to come to terms with losing Hope. Now Campbell was back and what was his first action? He went to see Hope in the middle of the day when he knew he was most likely to find her at home and on her own.

Andreas breathed in deep but the sick sense of rage threatening him did not abate. He leapt upright. Exactly what was he going to do? Go home. He rang his helicopter pilot and told him he needed to get there as soon as possible. Would it look odd if he just arrived back at Knightmere? He raked an uneasy hand through his cropped black hair. Hope might think he didn't trust her. He did trust her, he trusted her absolutely. But how could he possibly trust Ben Campbell?

Campbell might try to make a move on Hope. A guy didn't get over losing a woman like Hope that easily. Andreas knew that from painful personal experience. He had dumped Hope and lived in hell for endless weeks that were a blur of alcohol and misery. He did not want to go through that again *ever*. If Campbell attempted to lure Hope back to him, he was going to get a fight he would never forget.

On the top of the Nicolaidis building, Andreas boarded the helicopter. He felt out of control. That unnerved him. But he was quick to assure himself that there was no way he would lose his temper and get physical with Campbell. Hope would not like that and he was determined not to do or indeed say anything that might distress her. Possibly he should tell her how her seeing Campbell made him feel. He felt angry. He felt jealous. He felt threatened. Of course, he felt threatened! He was on like…continual probation. She wouldn't marry him. The one thing that would give him a sense of security, she denied him and she would not tell him why.

Maybe he should make a special effort to explain just how important she was to him. That was something he had always been careful to keep to himself, but now he was afraid that he had kept quiet for too long and missed his chance. She was very, very important to his peace of mind. He could not bear the idea that anything might ever harm her. He thought he was incredibly lucky to have got a second chance with her. Was that love? How was he supposed to know what love was? Before he had met her, he had never been in love. He was morosely convinced that Campbell wouldn't hang back from saying he loved her.

Hope tensed when she saw the helicopter coming in to land. Why had Andreas changed his plans and returned to the house? Was it because he was unhappy about Ben coming to visit? She really hoped it wasn't that.

'Andreas…' she murmured as he strode into the drawing room, his lean, strong face shuttered and taut. 'Did you forget something?'

'*Ne*…yes,' he breathed in Greek, his eyes smouldering gold as his expressive mouth curved into a smile that was purely for her.

'Let me introduce you to our visitors,' Hope said warmly.

Visitors in the plural? Disconcerted, Andreas turned his head and saw to his surprise that Ben had his arm wrapped round a tiny exquisite brunette. A perceptible air of intimacy clung to the other couple.

'Of course, you know Ben…this is Chantal,' Hope informed him.

Andreas extended a hand to Ben and kissed the brunette on both cheeks French style.

'I'm afraid we have to make tracks,' Ben told them. 'My mother's expecting us this afternoon.'

Having watched them drive away, Andreas closed a hand tightly over Hope's. 'I was really scared that Campbell was back to make a play for you,' he admitted half under his breath.

Hope dealt him a startled glance. 'Andreas…at this moment, I'm the size of a medium-sized house,' she pointed out gently. 'I don't think there's much risk of any guy making a play for me right now.'

'I've had a problem handling your friendship with him.' Dulled colour scored his high cheekbones. 'If you hadn't been pregnant, you'd probably still be with him—'

'No, slow up there!' Hope inserted in dismay. 'As far as I'm concerned I'm with you by choice and our baby has very little to do with it.'

'But you had something good going with Campbell—'

'I liked him very much but he's not you and he was never going to be.'

Encouraged by that statement, Andreas bit the proverbial bullet. 'I've been jealous as hell—'

Hope looked up at him in amazement. 'But why?

There's no need. I had only started seeing Ben when I found out I was expecting. It's not as if I slept with him or anything like that!'

The silence sizzled.

'You...*didn't* sleep with him?' Andreas prompted fiercely. 'Have you any idea how much knowing that means to me?'

'If you had asked, I would never have lied. You didn't ask.'

Andreas flexed lean brown fingers, shrugged broad shoulders, compressed his beautiful mouth and nodded into the bargain. It took all those separate gestures to express the intensity of his response. 'It always meant a lot to me that I had been your only lover—'

'You never said.'

'I took you for granted. You were there. Life was good and then...pow! It's gone,' he breathed in a roughened undertone, pulling her close as though to combat that unhappy memory.

'Elyssa,' she sighed.

'Her lies tore me apart. I have never been so wretched in all my life. I didn't understand what you meant to me until you were gone,' Andreas confessed raggedly above her head, his strong arms tightening expressively round her. 'Then I couldn't admit to myself that I hated my life without you in it.'

'Honestly?' Her head came up, turquoise eyes focusing on him.

'Honestly.'

'But what about all the women you were seen about with?'

Andreas grimaced. 'Window dressing.'

Hope snatched in a stark breath. 'Did you undress any of the windows?'

Andreas winced. 'Couldn't...'

Her eyes rounded. '*Couldn't?*'

'I couldn't because...' Andreas dragged in a sustaining breath before he pushed himself on to the crux of the matter. 'I couldn't because I only turn on for you. Didn't you notice how hot I was for you at the cottage?'

'You've been faithful.' A huge sunny smile lit up her heart-shaped face.

'I'll always be faithful...' Andreas hesitated. 'I love you, *pedhi mou.*'

Her lashes fluttered up on wide, disbelieving eyes.

'It's true...I do!' Andreas stressed as if she had argued the score with him. 'When I feel this weird, it's got to be love!'

'You love me...' Hope felt buoyant with happiness. 'I love you too—'

'So why won't you marry me?' Andreas demanded fiercely. 'Being single is driving me mad!'

'Oh, I think I could do something about that and save your sanity for you,' Hope whispered teasingly. 'If you love me—'

'I love you like crazy!' Andreas launched, cupping her cheekbones with his spread fingers.

'I'll marry you just as soon as you can get it organised,' she told him happily. 'That was what I was waiting and hoping for. I didn't want you to marry me unless you loved me.'

Andreas did not let the grass grow under his feet. The relatives assembled to meet Hope that weekend extended their stay and got treated to a big splashy wedding in Athens. Hope's grasp of the Greek language was finally revealed and much admired. Hope took centre stage in a pink off-the-shoulder dress and a bag in the shape of a lucky horseshoe. Vanessa acted as her bridesmaid. Ben attended with Chantal. The paparazzi turned out in large numbers but were prohibited any wedding pictures by tight security arrangements.

The happy couple returned to Knightmere for their honeymoon because the bride did not feel up to anything more strenuous. When she lamented that truth, Andreas just laughed and reminded her that they had their whole lives in front of them.

Karisa Nicolaidis was born five weeks later. Andreas had to get Hope to the hospital in the middle of the night, an event he had planned for with split-second timing. It was an uneventful and quick delivery. Karisa came into the world at dawn with her mother's lack of fuss. With her crisp head of dark curls, she was a very pretty infant and she was christened when she was four weeks old.

Elyssa sent a gift. Andreas returned it without discussing the matter with Hope. When Hope found out, she told Andreas that she thought it was time that hostilities ceased. By all accounts, Elyssa was having a rough enough time. Her husband, Finlay, was divorcing her and contesting custody of their two little boys. Hope encouraged Andreas to at least consider the idea of speaking to his sister again as, while he was unwilling, Elyssa was receiving the cold-shoulder treatment from most of his family.

The collection of bags that Hope designed for Leonie Vargas sold like hot cakes and catapulted her name to fame. Instead of being called the 'bag lady' by the press, she was referred to as the 'reclusive accessory designer, Hope Nicolaidis.' Her bags sold for a small fortune. Andreas was impressed to death by her profit margins but he never did comprehend the attraction of most of her designs.

Several months after the birth of their daughter, Andreas flew Hope to Paris for a very special meal. When they got back to their exclusive hotel suite he presented her with a fabulous pair of diamond earrings. 'This is our third anniversary since we met, *agape mou.*'

After a night of wild passion they lay talking way into the small hours. Curved beneath his arm, Hope loosed a blissful sigh. 'I'm so happy...'

'And I intend to devote the rest of my life to ensuring that you stay that way,' Andreas promised, his dark golden eyes full of love resting on her smiling face.

The world's bestselling romance series.

HARLEQUIN®
Presents
Seduction and Passion Guaranteed!

Back by popular demand...

EXPECTING!

She's sexy, successful and PREGNANT!

Relax and enjoy our fabulous series about couples whose passion results in pregnancies... sometimes unexpected!

Share the surprises, emotions, drama and suspense as our parents-to-be come to terms with the prospect of bringing a new life into the world. All will discover that the business of making babies brings with it the most special love of all....

Our next arrival will be

HIS PREGNANCY BARGAIN by *Kim Lawrence*
On sale January 2005, #2441
Don't miss it!

THE BRABANTI BABY by *Catherine Spencer*
On sale February 2005, #2450

www.eHarlequin.com   HPEXP0105

The world's bestselling romance series.

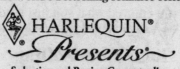

Seduction and Passion Guaranteed!

They're the men who have everything—except a bride....

Wealth, power, charm—what else could a heart-stoppingly handsome tycoon need? In the GREEK TYCOONS miniseries you have already been introduced to some gorgeous Greek multimillionaires who are in need of wives.

THE GREEK BOSS'S DEMAND
by *Trish Morey*
On sale January 2005, #2444

THE GREEK TYCOON'S CONVENIENT MISTRESS
by *Lynne Graham*
On sale February 2005, #2445

THE GREEK'S SEVEN-DAY SEDUCTION
by *Susan Stephens*
On sale March 2005, #2455